The Trouble
with Romance

Book 2, The Cupid Series

by

Tamara Philip

Vanilla Heart Publishing

The Trouble with Romance
by Tamara Philip

Published by: Vanilla Heart Publishing
www.VanillaHeartPublishing.com
10121 Evergreen Way, 25-156
Everett, WA 98204 USA

ISBN-13: 978-069238-26-15   ISBN-10: 0692382615

10 9 8 7 6 5 4 3 2 1 First Edition

First Printing, February 2015
Printed in the United States of America

The Trouble
with Romance

Book 2, The Cupid Series

by

Tamara Philip

Table of Contents

Dedication

For Natalie Gilbert

Thank you for not giving up when I was more than ready to.
All eight times. Love you.

Acknowledgements

I'd like to thank my mom and dad, Debbie and Franklyn, for their endless support and ignoring my manic outbursts which were quite frequent,

My fiancé, Chris Vaughan, for causing most of those manic outbursts and yet somehow still being wonderful,

Jane Vaughan, Thank you for our rants about literally everything and being you,

My sisters Tamiko, Tanyakka and Tulani, who are amazing soundboards and genuinely awesome people,

My Author BFF, Neva Squires Rodriguez who is honestly everything an author should be,

My gorgeous niece, Meilani for being an absolute delight,

and Zeath Jackson, for being the kind of person that reminds you that there is beauty in the world.

Chapter One

"Your boyfriend is a lunatic and I'm going to need him to never ask me for a favor again! I value my life too much for that!" Clarissa exclaimed the very second her best friend climbed into the front passenger side seat of her silver SUV.

"Uh oh, what did Tom do this time?" December giggled as she pulled her seatbelt across her chest.

Nearly a year later and she still blushed whenever anyone called Tom her boyfriend. Who would have thought that she, December Brown, aspiring recluse, would not only be dating the man of her dreams but also living with him! Regardless of the fact that she was a bona fide pop star with six platinum selling albums and countless magazine covers under her belt, it never truly resonated with her that she was a celebrity dating another celebrity. She simply felt like the luckiest girl in the world whose boyfriend happened to be one of Hollywood's hottest actors and voted The World's Sexiest Man two years running.

"Don't laugh! I was really terrified! Tom Elmswood should be banned from every type of motor vehicle in the universe!"

"Oh my God, you let him drive didn't you? I warned you! I said don't fall for that puppy dog look he gives!"

Tom just happened to also be the world's most hazardous driver. December cackled loudly at Clarissa's horrified expression.

"I didn't stand a chance, Dee! It's not funny! He showed up all early with breakfast! You know that's our downfall! Damn you egg and cheese on a roll." Clarissa grinned at her as she put her car into drive.

"Mmm...I could go for one right now! Ronnie has me on an evil master cleanse! I haven't eaten solids in four days!" December lamented.

"I know it sucks, but you do have a music video to shoot this week and Tom's movie premiere to go to! So, he's just looking out for you...you know how the tabloids are."

December sighed dramatically.

"I know but I'll probably starve to death before any of it at this rate! I need something covered with cheese and bacon! I need it to live!"

"Fine. You can order what you want tonight, but you have to swear not to tell your scary personal trainer about it."

"Yay! Okay, I promise. By the way, he was asking about you." December sang out, wiggling her eye brows suggestively.

"Ew, why?"

"Ronnie is not that bad. When he isn't starving me or yelling at me, he's pretty nice. But more importantly, he thinks you're hot. So, can I give him your number?"

"Absolutely not. He always looks like he stepped out of shower, but only if the shower was in a swamp." Clarissa shivered in disgust as December burst out laughing.

"Stop! I'm dying here. Be nice."

"Ugh, I know that's not all sweat so why is he constantly so moist?"

"I don't even know! Honestly, he always looks like that, even in normal clothes." She admitted once she stopped snickering.

"See? He's gross. Don't tell me that he doesn't look like a drowned rat."

They broke out into additional peals of laughter as Clarissa navigated her car through the traffic on the Triborough Bridge en route to their friend and December's stylist, Terrence Mitchell's, hair salon in East Harlem.

"So, Terrence told me you're going to do something different with your hair?"

"Yeah, I'm thinking honey brown with gold low lights." December answered, twirling a few strands of her curling dark copper hair.

Clarissa glanced at her best friend briefly and nodded. With the singer's own golden complexion, the combination of the two colors would only enhance her natural glow.

"Definitely. That'll look good with your skin tone. We're still going out to dinner tonight after, right?" It was hard enough getting everyone together in the same city these days, let alone organizing a dinner while Tom was in the middle of filming a new movie.

"Of course. Damien and Marilyn can't make it though, the baby is sick. So it'll just be us, Tom, Terrence and David." December responded as she frantically played Candy Crush on her phone.

"Aw poor little Sophie. I guess we'll have to have another dinner date when everyone can come."

"Maybe at my place so the baby can come along and just do take out?" December offered, her eyes still glued to the little rectangle screen.

"Actually, that sounds great. I'll put that into my calendar when we're at Terrence's. Anyway, I'll get Carl to swing by the restaurant afterwards to take some photos. I'll have him leak a few of them out to the tabloids."

"Who's Carl?" December asked, already making a face at the prospect of having to take pictures.

"The freelance photojournalist I have on speed dial. Basically he's a paparazzi that I've promised to give first dibs to anything to do with you as long as he plays by my rules and gives me a heads up on any negative headlines about you that he hears about through the grapevine."

"Oh, him. I know you can't see since you're driving and all, but I'm trying not to roll my eyes right now. Can't we just enjoy tonight without inviting photographers? What's the big deal about a dinner with a few friends?"

"First of all, people go wild for any footage of you and Tom out and about together. It's a perfect chance to show off your new hairstyle and give the public what they want, which is seeing you canoodling with Tom. You both need the publicity, especially with Tom's movie about to hit the theatres." Clarissa explained for what felt like the billionth time. She didn't mind all that much since things like this were the reasons behind her becoming December's agent; Clarissa thought about the bottom line while December just wanted to sing and then be left to her own devices.

"That's true. You're right, and I also get to see photos of us together that I would have never gotten on my own. Which is kind of awesome, right? Don't forget to call Maurice then."

"Of course. We're a pretty good team, Maurice and I. We're on the same wavelength about how to do our jobs, so that makes it much easier than I anticipated."

"Really? But Maurice is so um...emotionally distant. Isn't it just a check for him? I mean, you're my best friend, so you actually care about my feelings..."

"Maurice adores Tom. He's just like a son to him." Clarissa stated as if it were common knowledge. December furrowed her eyebrows in confusion.

"What? Are you serious?"

"Yup. He literally lights up every time he talks about him. His wife, Estelle, told me everything. How they lost their own son, Jeffrey, in a school bus crash when he was seventeen, and how Tom is so much like him and that it's hard for Maurice to show his feelings, but Tom's well-being is just as important to him as yours is to me." December's mouth hung open in shock.

"Holy...wait! Why doesn't Tom know any of this? He's only met Estelle like a handful of times in the 6 years he's worked with Maurice."

"Well, I've had a few meetings with Maurice since you two have started dating, and Estelle would swing by his office to bring him some lunch. We ended up chatting. You'd like her!"

"I'm so jealous right now! I've been trying to find a way to connect with Maurice for a while now, too. Okay, that's it! We'll have to invite them out for dinner or something."

"You can try but I don't know if they'll ever accept. I mean, it's hard for them because Tom resembles Jeffrey so much. Estelle actually cried when she told me that, but Tom's like a walking talking "what could have been" for them. It's still too hard for her to see him, but Maurice seems to find some solace in it."

"Oh my God, that's so sad! But...I get it now. He doesn't want to get too close because he knows there's a difference and it could get kind of creepy, I guess?"

"Precisely. Anyway, you don't have to worry with Maurice in Tom's corner. ...Please tell me those aren't tears in your eyes." Clarissa asked hearing the tell-tale wobbly lilt to December's voice. It wasn't hard to guess that the waterworks weren't too far behind.

"It's really sad, C!" December replied, wiping her eye with one hand and fanning her face with the other.

"I know, I know. I was misty-eyed too when I first heard it" she agreed, remembering her own reaction.

"Why didn't you say before? When did you find out?"

"Not so long ago, actually. Maybe a week or so? I kept forgetting to tell you with all the excitement of you getting nominated for Album of the Year and all."

"True! I don't even want to think about that craziness tonight. I just want to relax with my friends before we're all swamped with promoting." December fiddled with her cell phone, staring at her contact list longingly, the colorful game already forgotten.

"You're dying to tell Tom everything I just told you, aren't you?"

"Oh my God, yes! Is it that obvious? I don't know how I'll be able to keep it to myself before I explode." Her pretty face flushed with contagious excitement.

"Well, you can't just blurt it out on the phone!" Clarissa admonished, barely concealing a smile.

"I know! But seriously, this is huge, and it's going to blow Tom's mind!"

"Well, tell him tonight at dinner. It's only a few hours to wait. I think you can hold it in."

December begrudgingly agreed.

"Oh, crap, I think I just ran a red light. I mean, it only just turned red so it should be okay right? Clarissa asked worriedly.

"Yeah, totally. It happens."

The flashing lights coming up behind them alerted them that perhaps the law disagreed.

Chapter Two

"Of course it would be just my luck to have a police car behind me. Ugh. My registration is in glove box, can you hand it to me please?"

December silently did what she was told. She always felt very nervous whenever she was pulled over. As if she was on the run from some horrendous crime and the law finally caught up to her even though she had no priors and didn't even litter. She barely even jaywalked if she could help it, choosing rather to wait for the WALK sign before crossing the street.

"Dee, breathe. I might get a ticket at the most. It'll be fine, okay?" Clarissa soothed, reaching over to gently squeeze December's hand. Her eyes, however, were glued to the tall police officer striding towards her driver's side window. He knocked on her window and she exhaled deeply, slapped a smile on her face and pressed the button to lower it.

"Good afternoon, officer"

"Afternoon. You missed that red light back there." he replied gruffly, his eyes trained forward, as if the long stretch of road ahead was more interesting than anything in the car.

"I know! I'm sorry! I just realized it at the last minute and it was too late to reverse before the light changed to green."

"Uh huh. License and registration, please." Clarissa quickly handed it over, finally chancing a quick glance up at him. He wasn't classically gorgeous like Tom or Damien, December's bodyguard, or the stylishly preened perfection of Terrence. His nose was just a little on the pointy side, his hair was at least two weeks overdue for a haircut, and he had a brooding kind of look about him as if he'd seen it all, done it all and he was judging you for it. Nevertheless, the cop was still a very good looking man. His steel gray eyes framed enviously long dark lashes that only served to compliment his olive toned complexion, all of which was topped off with a sexy five o'clock shadow which piqued Clarissa's interest. She had a thing for ruggedly handsome men.

The policeman leaned down and tilted his head to peer into the car through the driver side window. His gaze stopped on the only other person in the car and his frowning face broke into a pearly white smile which looked a little like sunshine after a particularly cloudy day.

"You're December Brown, aren't you?" he asked in awe.

December's head snapped towards him, her eyes sparkling in sheer delight. Clarissa smiled to herself. After all these years, December was still surprised when someone recognized her in public.

"That's her, alright." Clarissa piped in.

He blinked at the sound of her voice and finally made eye contact for the first time, slowly scanning her face from top to bottom before landing back on her dark green eyes, then turning back to December. It was almost mechanical the way he assessed her and then dismissed her within seconds as if she was just a figment of his imagination.

"I'm a huge fan of yours, Ms. Brown! Were you speeding so you could meet with Tom Elmswood?" He asked, rather sweetly.

"Oh brother." Clarissa thought barely reining back the need to roll her eyes. Had December been behind the wheel, he'd have probably given her a police escort. Typical.

"I wish! I was going to my stylist to get my hair dyed before a going out to dinner with some friends. Tom is going to meet us there because he's busy filming an indie movie in Pennsylvania until much later." December blabbed unnecessarily.

Before she gave away state secrets, Clarissa decided to intervene.

"What's your name, Officer? Maybe December can give you an autograph?"

"Peter. Peter Bassano. Wait. Wait a minute...are you trying to bribe me?"

"Hardly. It's a signature on a piece of paper." Clarissa retorted, dryly. December shot her an alarmed look. Peter glanced down at Clarissa's license with a scowl.

"Ms. Gregory, what do you do for a living?" he asked coldly.

"I'm December's agent and publicist."

"She's also my best friend. Please don't arrest her." December piped in.

Peter's intense glare at Clarissa softened into one of adoration at December's pleading words.

"Of course not, Ms.Brown-"

"Call me December, or Dee, everybody does."

Peter's beam was so wide Clarissa could see he had one slightly crooked bottom row tooth.

"Okay, well, December, I'll give your friend a warning this time. But, she has to be more careful."

Clarissa opened her mouth to respond but December cut her off quickly.

"Of course, Officer Bassano."

"Peter." he corrected, eagerly.

"Are we free to go now?" Clarissa asked rudely. December shot her a "have you lost your mind look", which she shrugged off with an attitude.

"Don't mind Clarissa. I think she forgot her manners somewhere."

"Yeah. Sorry." She mumbled reluctantly. Peter ignored her half-hearted apology as he dug into his navy blue uniform shirt pocket before pulling out a black note pad.

"Would you sign this for me, December?"

"Sure, Peter. Do you want me to make it out to you?" she asked as she reached past an exasperated Clarissa to take the small notebook from him.

"No, can you make it out to Diana and say happy fifteenth birthday in it?"

"Aw, is that your daughter? You don't look old enough to have a kid that age."

Peter smiled "I'm thirty-two and she's not my kid. She's my god-daughter. Her birthday is tomorrow, and she'll be so happy when she sees your autograph."

"Oh! Well, jot down her address and I can send her a t-shirt or something?"

"Really? That would be fantastic. She's an even bigger fan than me. She's crazy about you."

"She's not the only one who's crazy." Clarissa grumbled.

"Yeah, she didn't say that. It was, the um... car engine?" December hurriedly explained with a horrified expression on her face.

Peter chuckled despite himself. He knew he should have been mad but that excuse was just...so bad.

"You should get that checked out. It sounds like it may have a brat under the hood." he remarked looking pointedly at Clarissa as December handed him the signed autograph.

"It was a real pleasure meeting you, December. Try not to miss any more red lights, Miss Gregory." He tapped the car as he walked back to his own.

Silence prevailed in Clarissa's car until the police car pulled out and drove off.

"What was that? Did you want to go to jail? What is wrong with you?"

"Nothing, he was just being really weird. He was pretty creepy. Didn't you think he was creepy, fawning all over you like that?" Clarissa replied, stubbornly. She was well aware that she reacted badly to him but his indifference truly bothered her in a way she couldn't explain.

"He was not. He was just being nice not arresting you and all."

"He wasn't going to arrest me for going past a red light."

"Fine a ticket, then. You didn't get a ticket and yet you were acting as if he was stalking us."

"I just wanted to go, and he wouldn't shut up."

"Oh my God, Clarissa. Were you jealous?" December asked, incredulously.

"Ew, as if! He wasn't even that hot." Clarissa protested, screwing her face up in disgust. December didn't buy it for a second

"He kinda was..."

"He was super annoying so that took away from any supposed attractiveness." Clarissa admitted, sourly.

"Uh huh. Well, he was just a fan, babe, and you were pretty mean to him."

"Blah!"

"...and I didn't even get his god daughter's address because of you!"

"Fine, what was his name again? Peter something? I'll do some checking and I'll send the t-shirt to his precinct. It's the least I could do since he didn't give me a ticket." Although she feigned ignorance at knowing his last name, Clarissa had already committed it to memory. Not that she would admit that to anyone.

"Yay, you're being nice again instead a jerk!"

"Hooray." Clarissa, deadpanned.

December's phone beeped with several messages.

"Uh oh, it's Terrence, demanding our location."

"See, I was right. That Peter guy sucked."

Chapter Three

"Voilá, you're all done and honey-dyed." Terrence spun her around in the hairdresser's chair to see her reflection in the mirror. December shrieked happily. Terrence Mitchell was a genius with his skill. The flawless makeup he'd applied complimented her new lighter hair color and had her looking photo-fabulous.

"Oh Terry, it's perfect! I couldn't ask for better." She fluffed out her shoulder length freshly-styled hair and admired all of his hard work.

December knew how lucky she was to have such a fashionable stylist like Terrence who not only did her hair and makeup effortlessly, but also designed her clothes and outfits so well that she constantly made the Best Dressed Celebrities lists.

"Glad you like it, Dee! I put your outfit for tonight in the back room. And don't even bother trying to argue. It would be pointless. Clarissa, get your cute butt into this chair! We have less than hour to get ready and get there and you all of a sudden want a layered look. Okay, girl, whatever."

Clarissa took her time walking over to where Terrence stood impatiently beside the newly vacant chair. She was in a foul mood and she didn't quite understand why, but everyone was getting on her last nerve. Normally, she would have sweet talked Terrence out of his justifiable reluctance with an easy banter but not today. She was feeling miserable and like the saying goes "misery loves company" and she was willing to spread hers around.

"If you don't think you can handle it, I can always find someone else to do it." Clarissa retorted, rather nastily.

Terrence's face contorted into an almost comical look of shock. Clarissa never spoke to him like this.

"And she never will again," he thought as he narrowed his eyes at her and bared his blindingly white teeth. "Excuse me, Clarissa? You want to repeat that?"

December rushed out of the dressing room just in the nick of time. She stood in between her two fuming friends, with only one shoe on. "Terry, put down the scissors. Please! She didn't mean that, she's just in a mood. A cute guy ignored her."

Understanding dawned in Terrence's eyes, although his impeccable eyebrows stayed arched in outrage.

"Oh! Yikes! Okay I'll let her slide this time but she was going to get a haircut she would never forget."

"I know, I know, and she was kind of asking for it. Weren't you, Clarissa?"

"Blah." she replied, petulantly. She folded her arms and slumped in her seat.

"We're adults, Clarissa. Please use your words." December scolded, biting her lip to hide her smile.

"Double blah."

"She's really taking this hard." December said, turning towards Terrence to hurriedly explain the meeting with Peter.

"Girl, he's a beat cop. I don't know why you're worrying about him. Do you know how much uniformed officers make?" Terrence scoffed, shaking his head.

"Not the point. Clarissa, what's wrong? It's not like you were flirting with him and he wasn't interested." December prodded, hoping to shake her out of her funk.

"I know that. I just...I don't know. I can't explain it. Maybe I'm lonely or something? I don't know. But you know what? I won't ruin today for everyone. I'm sorry, Terry. I am very sorry. Let's just get ready and have a great night, okay?"

Terrence and December exchanged fleeting looks but murmured sounds of agreement.

"Guess who?"

A large pair of male hands covered December's eyes. She giggled, already guessing who it was by his cologne and his voice.

"Trace! Oh my God! This is the best surprise!" she shrieked, yanking his hands off her face as she wrenched herself out of her seat to hug him.

"Hey, Dee. I missed you."

Trace rubbed her back lovingly as she clung to him. It was nearly six months since they'd last seen each other due to endless show business duties.

"I missed you so much, Trace. Thank you so much for coming tonight. What are you doing in town?" she asked, finally untangling herself from him.

"I'm Clarissa's date for the night, actually. She found out that my schedule had me in New York this week and forced me not to tell you. Where's the waiter? I need a drink. Where's Tom? Hi, everybody else!"

He beckoned over a waitress who was staring wide eyed at the talk show host. Trace expected this response not only because he was easily recognizable due to everyone watching his wildly popular celebrity chat show, Trace Randall Tonight, but also since the last time anyone saw December and Trace together was on his show. His cringe-worthy attempt at playing matchmaker to Tom and December still lived on in television infamy almost a year later. Trace couldn't live it down and, unfortunately, neither could Tom and December. Every time any of the trio's names were in the media someone always brought it up. Not to mention the rumors that still flew around that their relationship was a sham or a publicity stunt, no matter how many candid photographs were released.

"Filming ran late but he's on his way now." December explained, her eyes flickering to the restaurant's entrance before settling back on her friends who were now clamoring around Trace for the hugs and kisses.

"Oh, okay. Where's the menu? I'm having a steak and if anyone says the word 'macrobiotic', I will probably punch them." Trace threatened, looking around the table.

"December already banned the word 'diet' entirely from this table." Clarissa informed him as she busily typed on her smartphone. "By the way, there will be a few paparazzi outside when we leave to snap some photos so please be on your best behavior."

"So what you're saying is, don't spill steak sauce down the front of my shirt unless my jacket can cover it up when closed?" Trace asked sarcastically.

"Pretty much."

"Can you be my agent because someone should have told me that two months ago so I wouldn't have been on the cover of People magazine looking like a hobo and being fat-shamed." he grumbled bitterly, still reeling from the cruel media backlash.

"It was just a bad photo of you, Trace. You don't usually look like that." Terrence said, looking offended on his behalf. David and Clarissa nodded in agreement.

"I know, that's what I said, but my agent tossed me on insanity kick plus..."

December tuned out the rest of Trace's words when the restaurant door opened. She knew it was Tom before he even stepped through the doorway but forced herself to stay in her seat, albeit at the very edge of it, until she was absolutely sure. The second she saw his face though, she sprung out of her seat like a shot, tossing decorum to the wind and rushed to where he stood.

Tom's face beamed brightly when he saw December round the corner. He lifted her up as she launched herself into his open arms. His cheeks hurt from how wide he grinned. They'd only been apart for three days and yet that was still too long for them.

"Hi." she breathed into the crook of his neck as she inhaled his scent.

"Hey, gorgeous. You're blonde." He said through a mouthful of hair, hugging her tighter.

"Honey-brown," she corrected.

"Oh. Well, it looks great. And you look beautiful."

Tom let her down slowly, capturing her lips with his as he did so. She smiled against his mouth, her hand resting gently on his smoothly shaven face.

Flashes from cameras shook them from their publicly private moment, returning them to the fact that they were standing in the entry way of a restaurant, blocking the path, and leaving themselves exposed to onlookers who were armed with camera phones.

"Oops. Sorry about that! I was just so excited to see you and I have fantastic news about Maurice and I heard you tricked Clarissa into letting you drive her car. Also if she's mean to you, just ignore it. This cop ignored her and she's in a mood," December blurted out in a rush, as they took their time walking back to the table.

"Sorry, I've only heard like four words out of that. What happened to Maurice and Clarissa?" Tom asked, smiling indulgently at her. He took her hand in his and laid tiny kisses on the back of it. December blushed in delight.

"Sorry, I've been holding that in all afternoon! Okay so Maurice..." She began as they approached their friends but the jovial atmosphere that she left was no longer there.

Clarissa in particular looked pale and drawn, her shiny blonde hair stood out in stark comparison as it framed her face, hanging like bone straight sheets on either side. December quickly sat down in the chair closest to her, worry already etched in her face.

"Clarissa? What's wrong? Are you okay? What happened? What's wrong?" December asked, already on the verge of panic.

Clarissa never reacted to things like this. She took everything in stride. It had to be very bad for her to look so out of her depth.

"Dee, he's out on parole." Clarissa whispered, fearfully staring into her best friend's eyes.

Chapter Four

"No. Please...no." December's hand shakily covered her mouth in shock. She knew instantly who the 'he' in question was.

"Who? Who's out on parole? Tom asked, bewildered, searching their distraught faces for someone calm enough to answer the question. Only David looked just as lost as he felt.

"Darren Singh. Her stalker." Terrence finally answered.

"The one that broke into her hotel room while she was sleeping." Trace put in.

"And held her at knife point. Can't forget that part." Clarissa added bitterly.

"What? He did what? December? You never told me any of that." Tom turned to find her with her hand still covering her mouth, taking shallow breaths as she quietly hyperventilated.

"December, look at me," he said firmly, taking her face in both his hands but only haunted, dilated eyes look back in his general direction. Tom's heart clenched at how scared she was at just the mention of this man. He pulled her gently to him and wrapped his arms around her tense body, holding her until her breathing slowed down and she clung to him in return.

"December, I'm not going anywhere. No one is going to hurt you again. I'll sort them out if anyone dares to try." He continued to whisper soothing assurances as he stroked her hair.

Clarissa quickly filled him in on the details of how Darren's lawyer called her because she was the contact number to call for any changes regarding Mr. Singh's status, and that yes, he was sentenced to eight years for breaking and entering and aggravated assault, but got out early due to good behavior and prison overcrowding.

"Aggravated assault?!" Tom's eyes widened in alarm.

"I think December should explain that to you in her own time. For now though, I think that's enough news to handle." Clarissa advised gently, and stood up with her phone clasped in her hands. She leaned over to kiss the top of December's head and took a deep breath.

"I'm going to make a few calls. I'll be right back."

Once outside of the restaurant, she called Damien to alert him of the situation. She had him call in extra bodyguards to be around December at all times until the threat of Darren was considered neutralized, or at the very least, a restraining order or three. Clarissa shivered in the cold January evening but it wasn't the cold that bothered her as much as the thought of that lunatic being loose on the streets. She dreaded having to tell December and Tom that Darren's lawyer also informed her that he'd been fired within hours of his release, but she would have to soon enough. So now not only was he free, she no longer had anyone tracking him. Pacing back and forth in her stiletto boots, she wracked her mind at what to do.

"Think, Gregory, Think! How can you keep tabs on him?"

Clarissa's strongest talent was her strategic mind-set when it came to preparation, her absolute focus at being one step ahead of everyone else around her. She even had painted on her living room wall the words "To be forewarned is to be forearmed". Perhaps it was because she was raised by two parents who were in military intelligence, but even as a teenager, December used to jokingly call her Miss Batman due to the way she attacked every potential problem with a meticulous single-mindedness, from their carefully orchestrated first dates with the Andrews' brothers when they were fourteen, all the way to picking colleges. This gift only improved with age and the resources she now had available to her. It was safe to say that Clarissa Gregory was never one to leave things to chance, so leaving a psycho like Darren Singh, who caused her best friend so much pain, on the loose without a leash was not an option for her.

Her mind wandered to the police officer they'd met earlier when he'd pulled them over and she smiled to herself, sure that with his help she'd be able to ensure December and Tom's safety. First thing first though, she had to salvage what was left of their get-together.

Chapter Five

"Hi, may I speak to Officer Peter Bassano?"

Clarissa leaned over the front desk at the police station, craning her neck trying to catch a glimpse of the man in question in case he tried to escape.

The cop behind the desk gave her a wary look before sighing out an answer.

"He's no longer an officer, it's now Detective Bassano."

"Detective? What? No, you must be mistaken. I saw him only a few hours ago when he pulled me over for passing a red light and he was an officer. I'm talking blue uniform, patrol car, officer." She explained in disbelief. She received a withering gaze in response.

"Listen lady, I don't even know why I'm telling you this but his inter-department transfer went through and he's been promoted to detective. So either you want to have a seat and wait until he gets back to his desk or you can leave your number and he'll call you when he gets a chance."

"I'll wait."

"Fantastic. Please have a seat over there." he deadpanned.

Clarissa squinted to read the name above his badge.

"Thank you, Officer La Paglia"

"You're welcome. Seat. Have it." He didn't even bother looking back up as he pointed in the general direction he wanted her to retreat to.

After two hours of sitting uncomfortably between a drunken bear of a man who reeked of stale booze mixed with urine and a little old lady who didn't look all that innocent to be honest, Clarissa decided to give up and just speak to any free policeman currently in the station. But first she needed a large cup of coffee since it was nearly midnight and exhaustion was starting to set in. Clarissa had come directly to the police station after finding out which precinct Peter worked in, which was shortly after dinner was over and she'd sent everyone on their way. December hadn't said much throughout the remainder of the meal. She even ordered a salad and refused desert which was unheard for her, so they all knew that hearing the news affected her deeply.

Clarissa pushed the exit door open with her hip, already looking down at her phone for missed text messages when she collided with a solid mass.

"Sorry. Excuse me." She muttered without even glancing at who she bumped into; she simply kept on tapping at her screen as she walked away.

"Hey! It's you again. What are you doing here?" a vaguely familiar voice said from behind, causing her to stop in her tracks.

"Peter! I mean, Officer...uh, sorry...Detective Bassano. Just the man I wanted to see. Congratulations on the promotion, by the way."

Clarissa let out a huge sigh of relief. There was no way she could have slept knowing that Darren was out there, prowling around, unchecked. And although the thought was irrational, her intuition was telling her that Peter Bassano would be the correct man for the job.

"Thanks. How'd you find me?" Peter looked around as if expecting someone to jump out from behind her.

"Just made a few phone calls. I'm very clever." Clarissa admitted, pulling her coat closer to her body when an icy wind blew by, chilling her to the bone.

"I bet. Anyway, I was just about to head home for night. My shift is over." He said with a shrug, twirling his car keys in right hand.

"You can't. Not yet anyway. I need your help. Please. This can't wait until tomorrow. Please."

He stared at her for a long while. Long enough that she started to feel nervous under that stern granite gaze. She tugged at the ponytail that she'd haphazardly thrown her hair into, but never wavered as she stared back at him.

"Okay, Ms. Gregory, fine. It's pretty late. Why don't you come back inside and I'll get you some coffee and we can talk about whatever it is you came to see me about?"

"Oh, great! That would be great!" She stumbled towards the door feeling a little out of sorts.

No longer in his navy blue uniform, Peter wore regular street clothes and threw her for a loop. He went from a seven to a very sharp nine in his blue jeans and leather jacket. He towered over her 5'8' frame and that somehow made him seem even hotter.

"What are you like 6'2'?" she wondered aloud to herself.

"Actually, I'm 6'1'. It's just my broad manly shoulders make me seem bigger." he replied, tossing her a smug grin, causing her ears to heat up.

"Show off." she mumbled, looking away.

Leading Clarissa to a desk in the corner of the bustling police station amongst where many other officers and detectives were working, Peter offered her a chair before sitting down himself behind the desk.

"Okay, so how can I help you, Ms Gregory? It must be important if you waited around so late in the night to see me."

"It is. I appreciate you staying later so I'll just lay it out straight: this is about December. I need to put a restraining order out on a convict in her name, and I need to get in touch with his parole officer." Clarissa could tell she'd piqued his interest already.

"I'm sorry, but you're going to have to start at the beginning." Peter pulled out a pen and paper and started scribbling.

"I need you to know that we kept this out of the news and very quiet when it originally happened because we feared for December's frame of mind and how she would handle the media fallout if this was leaked to the press. So, I'm asking for discretion. Actually, no, I'm begging for it."

"Okay, I understand. I'll only be able to help you if I know everything. So start from the top."

"Well, about four years ago, December started receiving obscene phone calls, which we ignored before changing her phone number. Then very aggressive 'love letters' started arriving, from a man called Darren Singh. He lived in New Jersey at the time with his mother. Anyway, he became obsessed with her, showing up in places where he knew she would be because he'd tapped her phone lines. He's incredibly smart but completely creepy. We only found that out because it stopped looking like coincidences and started looking like it was planned, you know? Which he verified by leaving blatant hints in his letters."

"Do you have a copy of these letters still?"

"Yeah, I have them scanned here on this flash drive. But the originals are already in police records." She placed the little black memory stick in front of him on his desk.

"Okay, so now I understand the need for a restraining order but what does this have to do with his par..."

"No, that's not the reason for the restraining order. I mean, that's part of it but that's not the worst part. That happened about six months later when he followed her to her hotel after a concert in Minnesota. Now, this was in the beginning when she wasn't a pop star yet. She was still scratching out a name for herself in the music world, so we didn't have the need, nor really the resources, for constant security after a concert when she was only the opening act."

Peter nodded and jotted down some more notes.

"So, around three in the morning she heard a noise and woke up to find a strange man in her bedroom with a large knife. I think it was a Bowie. I don't know for sure. Everything else December has kept to herself all these years but the medical report is in there, sealed. I can say though that she may have been sporting a black eye but he was much worse off. She saved herself that night. He received ten years for aggravated assault and breaking and entering."

"I'm sorry she had to go through that."

"Yes, unfortunately he's out now due to overcrowding and good behavior. And the first thing he did was fire his lawyer so there's no way to track him on my end except through his parole officer."

"I can understand your concerns. Has he tried to make any contact with her as yet?

"No, but I don't want to give him the opportunity."

"I get that and I agree with what you want, but it's not really protocol to give out parolee's information to just anyone..." Peter explained, apologetically.

"Detective, are you telling me that she should be left unprotected?"

"No, not at all. What I'm saying is let me get the information you need by going through the proper channels. I'll call you as soon as I get it."

"Okay. What about the restraining order?"

"I'm all over that as well. Can you just give me any numbers and addresses I can contact you and December at?"

"Of course." Clarissa replied, already pulling out a manila folder with the information listed. "I've added our head of security, Damien Fimmel, who's the person you should talk to just in case you can't reach me. He's already ahead of the situation."

"Great. I just need to verify and get access to the files. I'm on the case, Ms. Gregory. Just try to be patient. Besides, he might just want a fresh start and to live trouble free so there's not much else we can do until I've made contact with his parole officer."

"I understand. I know he hasn't made any moves towards her yet but I just want to take these things as a precaution. You should have seen her today when I told her. She was so frightened."

"I'm sorry." Peter repeated, still as sincere as the first time. "You won't be flying blind again, if I can help it."

Clarissa smiled at him, relief seeping into her tired face. Peter smiled back.

"Here's my number. My cards don't come in until next week but you can call me day or night."

Peter scribbled it down on a piece of paper and handed her the paper. Their fingers brushed slightly as she took it from him, sending a tingle of shock where they touched. They stared at each other quizzically before simultaneously shrugging it off.

"Thank you so much for your help, Detective. Please call me as soon as you hear anything at all."

She turned to leave only to find him already at her side.

"I'll walk you to your car. It's late." He gestured for her to go first as he followed her out.

Peter trained his eyes forward, keeping the look of disinterest on his face. He forced himself to not look at the easy sway of her hips as he trailed behind her but it wasn't as easy as it normally was. Something about Clarissa was intoxicating to him. Damn his peripheral vision. He'd noticed her in the car's side view mirror as the moment he walked up to the driver side window. Her silky golden blonde hair and sparkling green eyes that held the tell-tale look of a shrewd mind. And her smile! Mischievous and sweet all rolled into one. It made sense that she was an agent. It made her even more attractive to him.

Too bad he didn't date anyone he met while on duty. It reeked of manipulation in his mind. How many people would say no to a cop who asked them out on a date while he was working on their case, without feeling a little intimidated? There would the fear that he wouldn't do his very best if they said rejected his advances.

As far as Peter was concerned that was just a line he didn't want to cross.

It didn't matter that his stomach did flips and twists each time Clarissa looked at him with her piercing gaze. So what if just the sound of her voice made his hands sweat and his pulse race like he was twelve again and she was his first crush? Clarissa never needed to know.

Besides, she seemed to have a lot on her plate; some guy trying to ask her for a date at a time like this would be all kinds of inappropriate, right? Peter rubbed the nape of his neck anxiously. He glanced Clarissa's way, only to catch her staring at him. She licked her bottom lip and Peter subconsciously mirrored her. He imagined they were as soft and pillowy as they looked.

"Get a grip, Bassano. Geez." He mumbled to himself.

"Listen, I'm sorry about earlier. I don't know what came over me and I was pretty rude to you." Clarissa said suddenly, breaking him out of his thoughts. She paused in front of her silver SUV, with her keys already in her hand.

"I should have given you the ticket." He remarked, gruffly. She scoffed in disbelief.

"You know, sometimes I think you have a sense of humor and maybe even a personality and then you act like a robot again."

Peter shrugged. Clarissa stared him, assessing him as if he were a new type of insect.

"If you lost the attitude you'd be a whole lot cuter."

"I think I'll survive." He smirked. "Have a good night, Clarissa. I'll call you if I hear anything."

She huffed, slamming her car door loudly as she got in, but it was better this way. There would be no conflict of interest if she despised him. And maybe those damned stomach flips would go away after a while if she did.

Chapter Six

The sound of retching woke Tom up in a start. He blearily stared around the nearly pitch black bedroom, trying to figure out where he was. After a few seconds, his eyes became accustomed to the darkness and he glanced over to see that December's side of the bed was empty. The sounds continued and he followed it to the sliver of light under the bathroom door. He listened silently with his hand on the doorknob but all he could hear now was quiet sobbing.

"December, are you alright?"

"Don't come in," she called out in a thin, glum voice.

"It's too late, I'm already turning the knob and coming in."

The bright light of the bathroom and the stark whiteness of the floor had him squinting all over again.

"Baby, what are you doing on the floor? Do you have food poisoning?"

"No," she said quietly with no plans to elaborate. She stared up at him with tears filling her hazel eyes and his heart broke for her all over again. He fell to his knees beside her on the cold tiles, pulling her to him as the sobs wracked her body again. She felt suddenly very fragile in her thin, sleeveless black silk nightie.

"Please talk to me, baby. You don't have to go through this alone. Please."

"I'm so scared, Tom. I got some weird texts earlier...what if it was from him? I can't go through that again." She croaked out after a while, bursting into tears once again.

"Shh, we'll get through this, sweetheart." Tom consoled her.

December clung to him even after the tears subsided, laying her head against his bare chest, listening to the calming sound of his steady heartbeats, sniffling quietly every once in a while. They sat on the bathroom floor until he felt her breathing slow down to an unhurried pace and he knew she'd fallen asleep. Tom shifted his body to prepare to lift her up when the phone rang. At the sound, she was up again, staring at him with impossibly wide terrified eyes.

"It's okay. I'll get it."

"No, no, no, no." she shook her head furiously, clinging to his arm.

"It'll be fine. You can come with me. I won't leave you." Tom said soothingly.

"It's him. It's him. I know it is." she whispered, shivering violently at the thought.

"It's probably just Clarissa worrying over you like I am."

December nodded reluctantly and loosened her death grip slightly when the answering machine picked up the call. Heavy breathing echoed throughout the large apartment. December froze on the spot.

"Did you miss me?" A darkly menacing voice moaned out, "'Cause I missed you."

The click of the call disconnecting uprooted her from her spot and she ran back to the toilet to throw up once again. Tom, on the other hand, was filled with a sort of wild, frantic rage; a feeling he wasn't familiar with but one he didn't think he'd ever forget.

The sound of his girlfriend vomiting in fear only fed into that rage. He picked up the phone to look at the number but when he tried to ring it back, it never connected.

He called Damien and told him about the call and to disconnect that phone number; he was to only contact them through his phone. After unplugging the phone from the outlet, he grabbed his and December's robes, phones and a blanket and headed back to the bathroom. He forced himself to seem calm for her sake. He knew she needed him now more than ever but there was a white hot rage burning feverishly in his belly now with Darren Singh's name on it.

When December slept for an hour straight without waking up, Tom carried her bridal-style back to bed. He was tired but sleep eluded him so he decided to lie beside her, watching her sleep for a while. December's caramel skin was sallow with dark circles under her eyes. Tom frowned, wanting to kiss away her pain but didn't dare in case it startled her awake. He padded quietly out of the room and closed the door. Putting the coffee on to brew, he stared out of the kitchen window contemplating how he was going to broach the subject to December without sending her spiralling into hysteria, when he felt her arms snaking around his waist. She kissed his back and hugged him tighter.

"I tried not to wake you."

"You didn't. I smelled the coffee and my stomach rumbled."

Tom caressed her face as she forced herself to smile brightly up at him. December wanted to hide away but she also didn't want to worry him any more than she had already.

"I'll make you an omelette. Would you like that or french toast? Maybe some cerea-" He offered, awkwardly, not knowing what to say.

"Baby, stop! I want all of the above actually but I'll accept eggs with toast so you won't judge me later on in life."

Tom laughed and kissed the tip of her nose. Maybe there was hope yet that she'd battle through these feelings and come out on top.

"Tom, I'm so sorry about last night. I, I just need a little more time and then I'll tell you everything, okay?" He grabbed her hand and placed it over his heart.

"I'm here whenever you're ready and even if you aren't ready. I love you and I'm not going anywhere."

"I love you, too. Thank you for being wonderful." December replied, finally smiling genuinely.

"Go watch some TV while I make us some breakfast. Clarissa will probably be here soon enough to check on you."

"It's four in the morning. I doubt that." she said through a loud yawn, followed by a full body stretch.

"Well, I called Damien last night after...the phone call."

"Oh my God, you did? I have to call her. She'll be climbing the walls!" She rushed over and picked up the house phone only to discover there was no dial tone. She gave Tom a confused look.

"I unplugged it last night. Use your mobile." He offered as he cracked an egg into a bowl.

"No."

"No?"

"I just, I... can I borrow yours please?"

"Um, sure...but what's wrong with yours?"

"The phone is ringing." December mumbled, obviously stalling. She headed back to their bedroom and shut the door. Tom quickly washed his hands and unlocked her cell phone. Twenty unopened text messages from the same unknown number. He scrolled below that and saw that she'd seen some of the earlier text messages from the same caller. He glanced at the still closed bedroom door and clicked on a message.

"What did the messages say?" Clarissa asked as she quickly put on her coat. After Damien called her, she'd nearly had her own nervous breakdown. It was just as she'd feared. She wanted to rush over to December's apartment like she usually would in any crisis, but Clarissa forced herself to stay where she was. Things were different now. December had Tom and although it took some getting used to after he'd moved in, Clarissa was happy that December was happy. It didn't hurt that Tom was easy-going and effortlessly fit into their makeshift family unit. Right now though, common courtesy was going out the window and she was going to comfort her best friend at four in the morning and no man nor beast was going to stop her.

"Just like random letters or something. It's so stupid. I'm probably overreacting again but it was late and I was still so worked up from earlier. I kept remembering everything I tried to forget for all these years. I just freaked...freaked out. It was a mess." December confessed in a rush.

Clarissa's mind was racing. Memories of four years ago came flooding back. Another late night call, the sound of ambulance sirens, police lights flashing and December. Oh God, Clarissa groaned suddenly feeling weak at the memory of December's bruised face and of holding her during the months of night terrors that followed.

"Detective Bassano is on the case, Dee! He promised he'd do his very best to make sure Darren stays away from you. Damien is also sending extra security detail to be with you around the clock." Clarissa replied, reassuringly. She decided to ditch waiting for the elevator and take the stairs so she wouldn't have to disconnect the call.

"Who's Detective Bassano? Wait...no way." December gasped in delight.

"Don't start. Anyway, I went to see him and found out he got a promotion, and yeah, now he's better able to help us." she explained as she connected her cell phone to her car speaker before pulling out of her parking spot.

"You like him." December sang, obnoxiously.

"Pfft, yeah right! Besides he's such a big fan of yours." Clarissa mimicked. "I figured he could actually be helpful instead of just star struck."

"Uh huh. You want to kiss him."

"Oh my god, shut up." Clarissa sputtered out a laugh, but admitted that he was actually very helpful when she saw him at his precinct.

"That's good. He looks like one of those heroic cops on Law and Order." December replied sleepily.

"None of them are that good looking though. Besides he's kind of a jerk."

"I don't know since I haven't seen an episode in years. Anyway you love a challenge. So are you going to call him about...tonight?"

"I left that to Damien. I don't want seem like I'm interested or anything, you know?"

"So you do like him!" December prodded, sounding more awake.

"Ugh aren't you supposed to be too upset to be in my business?"

"Never."

"I'll be at your place in less than ten minutes since traffic is pretty much non-existent at this time of the morning. Sit tight, babycakes. Let Tom spoil you until I get there."

"Thank you, C, for being consistently amazing."

"I love you." Clarissa replied, feeling emotional. For all the ups and downs throughout the years, she wouldn't have traded their relationship for the world.

"Love you too, see you soon." December said before ending the call.

Chapter Seven

"So I was thinking..." Tom mused, looking slightly unsure of how to broach a possibly touchy subject. December studied his face as she chewed a slice of buttery toast. She'd been expecting him to say something after she finished talking to Clarissa and came back into the kitchen. He'd seemed preoccupied as he set breakfast on the table.

"About?"

"Why don't you come stay with me while I film for a few days? My trailer has more than enough space and we'll get to spend more time together and..."

"Tom..."

"No, hear me out. I have to go back this evening or else I'll never hear the end of it but I also can't leave you knowing that absolute creep is hanging about. I need to keep you safe, and if I'm not with you, I'm not going to be able to concentrate. I know you have your video to film but we could be back in time for that."

"Tom, stop for a minute! Just breathe." He obliged her by exhaling loudly.

"Okay now listen, I would love to come with you for a few days."

"Really?"

"Yup. I was planning on hiding in your knapsack when you were leaving anyway."

"This is great. I thought I was going to have to toss you over my shoulder and drag you off to Pennsylvania against your will."

"Kidnapping is illegal, Thomas." she teased.

"I don't care." He said leaning over to kiss her briefly. "I'll do whatever it takes to keep you safe."

Before December couldn't respond, someone knocked on their front door.

"Finish eating, I'll get the door." He navigated his way to the living and unlocked the door to let Clarissa in. She gave him a quick hug, her eyes already searching for December.

"How's she doing?" She asked him quietly, noting his tired face and bedraggled hair.

"She's going to go back with me when I leave tonight. Just for a few days."

"I think that's a great idea, Tom. Damien and the police are now involved, so this is being handled, okay? But you should give Maurice a call. Let him know what's going on and what not."

"Yeah, yeah you're right. I'll call him now." he said rubbing his hand down his face.

"Go get some rest, you look terrible."

"Thanks," he replied, chuckling. "I'm going to take a quick shower."

"Okay, take your time." Clarissa headed towards the sounds coming from the kitchen.

"I'm going to assume this plate of eggs is for me." she announced, causing December to jump.

"Geez, you nearly gave me a heart attack. I think I nodded off for a second. "

December opened her arms wide and Clarissa gladly stepped in to the embrace. They were nearly the same height, with less than a quarter inch difference between them. Both had curvy athletic figures and mirrored each other in so many ways, it sometimes felt like they were cut from the same cloth.

"If you cry I'll cry so don't even think of starting." Clarissa admonished, a stray tear already escaping down her face.

"I think I'm all cried out, actually. I know you haven't told me everything so just give it to me straight. Can I or can't I file a restraining order against him?"

"I have Detective Bassano on that, and Damien is on his way to collect the answering machine tape and your cell phone. As soon as we find out anything, I'll tell you. I promise."

"I know. I just feel so helpless."

"Did you tell Tom about the text messages?"

"No, but I think he knows. I refused to use my cell, and he picked up on that so he must have checked or assumed. I don't know."

"Where's your phone?"

"I don't kno- oh it's near the toaster. Hold on a sec, I'll grab it." She handed it over to Clarissa who quickly unlocked it, her eyes widening as she scrolled.

"How many messages did you say he sent you?"

"Maybe three or four before I lost it."

"Dee, there has to be at least twenty more texts here."

"What?!" She cried out in shock, reaching out for her phone.

"Don't delete any of them. It might be helpful to the police for the restraining order."

"I can't handle this, Clarissa. I won't live in fear again. How could anyone let this, this horrible creature out of jail?" She shrieked, visibly forcing herself to stop shaking.

"Calm down, Dee!"

"I am calm. I need you to get me a prepaid phone as soon as possible, please. I can't even look at this one without my stomach turning so I'm selling it and my answering machine. Whatever I get for them, I'll triple it then donate the money to charity. "

"Okay, that sounds reasonable. I'll get my personal assistant to do that."

"Thank you. I just don't understand how he's hacking in to my phones already. I thought he only just got out."

"He dropped out from MIT, so he's not just evil, he's very smart, too."

"When will Damien be here? I need to know he hasn't somehow bugged my apartment. I really don't want to have to move."

"You're not moving. It was a nightmare to get this place the way you want it. Don't you even think about it."

"That's true. Well I better get dressed and start packing. Did Tom tell you?"

"Yeah, he did. I agree entirely. While you two are away, we can get everything sorted out. I'll rearrange things with Ronnie so he'll meet you in Pennsylvania. I'll find the nearest gym and you can do your workouts there. Don't worry, you'll have a body guard wherever you go from now on. "

"Okay. If Darius is available, it would be great to get him. I trust him."

"I'll let Damien know as soon as he gets here. "

"You should call Peter. He can come here and rendezvous with Damien and his team."

"Good idea. And here I was thinking I was the brains in this duo."

"Oh, shush."

Chapter Eight

"Bassano."

"Hi Detective, it's Clarissa Gregory. December Brown's agent. I apologize for calling so early." Clarissa really didn't want to have to speak to him after their last meeting but this was more important than her pride.

"No worries, Ms. Gregory. I was just about to call you. I have good news and bad news." He answered, in a crisp, clipped way belying his increased heart rate at the sound of her voice.

"I need some good news this morning."

"Well, I'm holding in my hand right now a signed restraining order against Mr. Darren Singh, as well as his parole officer's information."

"Oh, that is fantastic news. Thank you so much." Clarissa gushed.

"No thanks necessary. If it wasn't for Damien's call a few hours ago, I wouldn't have been able to get the restraining order done so fast. After the phone-, after Mr. Singh made contact, it gave probable cause to request December's phone records which showed that the call did indeed originate from his listed whereabouts according to the parole board."

"Well, he also sent her multiple text messages to her cell phone. That should prove that he's already violating his parole, right?"

"There's bad news too, Ms. Gregory."

"Call me Clarissa and just give it to me straight, Detective."

"Well Clarissa, the thing is Darren Singh hasn't checked in with the parole officer. Nor was he at his last known address. The officers sent to that location found it ransacked but empty of all his belongings."

Clarissa felt faint, her legs suddenly rubbery. She grabbed hold of the kitchen island for stability as she let Peter's news sink in. Her mind went blank. From somewhere far away she vaguely heard Peter saying her name. He was still talking but she couldn't make out a word he was saying. How could she tell December that even with the help of the police, she had no guarantees that her stalker wouldn't try to contact her again?

"I failed her." She whimpered, hot tears brimming in her eyes.

"You didn't fail her, Clarissa. We're going to find him. Just have faith." Peter's deep voice resonated with sincerity and despite herself, Clarissa desperately wanted to believe him. She took a steadying breath.

"How soon can you get to December's apartment? Our security team is about to meet up within the next thirty minutes or so."

"I'll be there. It would be good to work together on this for when we find him. And we will find him." Peter vowed, hanging up shortly afterwards.

"I get that living in a movie trailer for a week is little daunting but think of it like camping." Tom's disembodied voice called out as the bedroom door opened, allowing December to step out fully dressed in jeans and a red oversized knitted sweater.

"I am and that's why I think we can stay in a hotel." She grumbled, seeming less than impressed with their current conversation.

"So you're saying you don't want to spend a few measly days in close quarters with me, the love of your life?" He followed her out while still yanking his long sleeved t-shirt over his disheveled short black hair. The navy color of his top only served to make the baby blue of his eyes even more striking.

December paused on her way to the living room to check him out. She couldn't help it. Even when was driving her up the wall, he still took her breath away. Tom caught the look she was giving him and smirked at her.

"I'm sorry, what are you two talking about?" Clarissa questioned, sticking her head out of the kitchen.

She positioned her face from her friend's direct line of sight, knowing December would pick up on her red rimmed eyes and general upset if she didn't.

"Ooh, Clarissa! Listen to this: I just calmly asked Tom if maybe we should stay in a hotel for a day or two. Just to break up the monotony of living in a rectangle box for seven days and he's trying to convince that it'll somehow be a romantic adventure." December explained in disbelief, as if it was an automatic given that nobody in their right mind would want to do what Tom suggested.

The Trouble with Romance

Clarissa chuckled despite herself; she needed the break from all of the negativity going on behind the scenes. Knowing that after the night the couple had just dealt with, they needed to let off steam somehow. If having a mini argument about something so trivial helped then she would humor them by playing along.

"That's right. And apparently, she disagrees entirely by the look of disgust on her face at the very idea." Tom's eyes twinkled in amusement. All he had to do was keep answering and December would take the bait.

"It's like my boyfriend has been abducted by aliens and they brainwashed him into thinking he's Bear Grylls or something. What next? Should we get a dog next?"

"Why not? What's wrong with that?"

"See! When we first got together, we were on the same page. The outdoors was something other people did. And pets? Thomas, think of the fleas!" December cried out overdramatically.

She flung herself on the overstuffed couch and covered her face with a fluffy purple cushion.

"Okay, I'm refereeing before we have to get smelling salts out for our Ladyship. Tom, what's going on? Are you secretly into camping now? And what about the fleas?" Clarissa inquired, not even bothering to hold back a grin.

"I've never been, I just thought it would be a laugh. Besides, I hardly think living in a decked out trailer on a closed film set counts as toughing it out in the wilderness." Tom answered, shrugging. Honestly, he still agreed with December about the outdoors and he was actually very worried about the fleas.

"See, Dee? Nothing to worry about. I'm sure Tom will realize how terrible it is to live in cramped quarters with you when you start complaining about every single thing under the sun. Especially since you'll still be on Ronnie's master cleanse. He's been so lucky that he's missed most of it this past week." Clarissa stated helpfully.

"Master cleanse?" He wondered softly, looking slightly horrified.

"Yup, I'm hungry all the time and all I can have is clear vegetable broth." December chipped in, shuddering.

"But you hate broths. You said consommé was the Devil's soup." Tom said, bewildered.

"It is and I still do." She nodded with unbridled glee on her face.

It took all of Tom's theatre school training to keep a straight face while she looked so happy. He wanted to slide his fingers through her tousled curly tendrils and kiss her face off in that moment, but he didn't want to give in so easily.

"What have I gotten myself into?" He muttered, shaking his head as he sat down next to her, lifting her blue jean clad legs and resting them on his lap. December smiled at him in the most patronizingly, sympathetic way possible.

"I'll make reservations for the weekend, then." Clarissa mused out loud, wandering back into the kitchen.

"So I heard you were doing some late night texting." Damien joked, causing the living room filled with six bodyguards, one police officer, two celebrities, and an agent to glare at him.

"Too soon?" He asked, looking around the room with an unapologetic, mischievous grin.

"And in poor taste, you big jerk." December responded, hitting him in the face with a striped cushion. He laughed and scooped her up in a bear hug. She hugged him back, knowing it was Damien's way of coping with the situation by breaking the ice.

He trailed after her as she worked her way over to the kitchen to get refreshments ready.

"Trace had to go back to Vancouver but he offered the services of these two gentlemen as additional security detail until this creep is caught. And he sends his love and regret that he couldn't stay."

"That was really nice of him. I'll call him later. How's Sophie feeling?"

"Better. It was her first ear infection. I think it was rougher on us than on her to be honest." Damien replied, as he opened the refrigerator in search of orange juice.

Peter hovered around the entrance to the dining room, looking slightly uncomfortable. He couldn't keep his eyes off of Clarissa who sat at the table studiously ignoring him by pretending to be busy typing on her phone. December shook her head in dismay at their awkwardness. She didn't have any experience in playing matchmaker but how hard could it be?

"Hey, Peter. Thanks so much for coming. Clarissa told me you were off duty and yet you're still here. You don't know how much I appreciate it." December said sincerely, placing a mug of hot coffee into hands.

"Anything for my favorite singer." He replied with a fond smile.

"He's so sweet. Isn't he sweet, Clarissa? So where are you taking your girlfriend on Valentine's Day?" She queried in a slightly too loud voice.

Clarissa rolled her eyes. Peter bit his lip to keep from laughing at her lack of subtlety.

"Uh, I don't have a girlfriend."

"Oh, that's very interesting. Isn't it, Clarissa?" December asked, staring pointedly at her friend. She even wiggled her eyebrows for effect.

"If I push you out of a sixth floor window, I can claim I was provoked." She intoned, the tips of her ears reddening slightly. Peter's smile widened.

Clarissa didn't embarrass all that easily; coming from a large family with many opinionated people didn't allow for that. Rejection didn't faze her much either. She'd developed a thick skin over the years as a young female agent making a name for herself in the sometimes brutal music industry. She wasn't even thirty yet and she was an agent coveted for both her fierce loyalty and meticulous ruthlessness. Running away wasn't even an option.

Yet here she was wishing she could hide away in embarrassment because her big-mouthed best friend couldn't help trying to meddle with a guy who was obviously not interested in her.

Clarissa refused to look up from her screen, fearing the look of utter disgust on his face. It wasn't that hard since she was playing one of the dozens of Facebook games she was addicted to playing. She was one of those annoying players who kept sending everyone on her friend list two million invites a day without any care that no one else was playing that particular game. So naturally, everyone who personally knew her quietly unfollowed her. She was a social pariah on that particular social networking site. Even December had to do it.

That didn't faze her either. It kept her looking busy and really isn't that what it's all about?

"Add me on CaféVille." Peter said, peeking over her shoulder. She hadn't noticed when he moved behind her.

"You play?" Clarissa asked, incredulously. Only December's adoptive mother, Sister Florence, also known affectionately as Nunny by December, had an account but she never checked on her café so she didn't really count.

"I'm on level eighty nine. It's kind of my thing." Peter bragged, dragging a dining chair over to where she sat.

"I'm on ninety. I guess I could add you." She said begrudgingly, secretly relishing the fact he was into Facebook games as well.

"Ugh, now there are two of you! I'll add you Peter but I swear I'm going to unfollow you two seconds later." December groaned.

"Hey, you play Candy Crush, so you can't judge." Clarissa pouted.

"Which is literally the only game you don't play so..."December shrugged, whipping out her phone to accept Peter's friend request.

"Do you hear the way she talks to me? Unbelievable." Smirking Clarissa turned to Peter to share in her mock outrage. He winked at her, setting butterflies loose in her tummy. She looked away, biting her lip.

"Peter, I just wanted to thank you personally for helping us out. We greatly

appreciate it." Tom said patting him on the back.

"Hey man, no worries, just doing my job." Peter responded, trying to play it cool, like he knew tons of celebrities and it was no big deal. It was mind blowing how quickly his uneventful life changed in less than twenty four hours.

"Clarissa told us that you've been promoted to Detective. That's fantastic. Congratulations."

"Thanks, I worked my butt off to get it. Great timing too, I guess huh?" He gestured vaguely to their surroundings. Tom nodded in agreement, taking the seat next to him.

"Lucky for us actually, right Clarissa?" Tom added with a not so subtle wink her way.

"You're severely allergic to peanuts, aren't you?" She replied, narrowing her eyes at him.

"Tom, stop bothering Clarissa. Clarissa, quit threatening Tom." December tossed out as she wandered back into the room with a large serving plate filled with granola bars and assorted fruits.

Peter chuckled, resting his arm on the back of Clarissa's chair.

"Okay, so do you guys have Darren under surveillance or something?" December asked, sitting down besides Tom at the dining table after gathering the rest of the group into the room. She looked pointedly at Peter then Damien. Peter glanced at the side Clarissa's guilt ridden face, quickly figuring out that she hadn't told December the news. He sympathized with her, realizing how hard it would be to have that conversation.

"We're working on that. There's an APB out for him in both New York and New Jersey. However, currently we are not aware of his whereabouts." He admitted, steeling himself against the possible hurled accusations and anger that normally accompanied an answer like that.

Tom crossed his arms, fighting a losing battle to keep a neutral expression. He was incensed and wanted to lash out. Then, from the corner of his eye, he caught sight of December's trembling hands. Reaching over, he covered them with his own, lending some comfort.

"Damien and Peter will be working together from now on, so you don't have anything to worry about, okay?" Clarissa added, reassuringly.

"Thank you, everyone, for your hard work. I need to go finish packing now." December announced, storming into her bedroom. A second later, she came back into the living, her hands balled in to angry fists as she stood in front of everyone.

"What's the plan exactly? What happens the week after when Tom goes to New Mexico to film his big battle scene? I can't go with him because I have charity events that I will not cancel. What are we going to do then? Or are we just going to wing it?" When no answers were forthcoming, she continued:

"I will be back in the city next week, like it or not. I'll stay with you, Clarissa, if you'll have me. If nothing is resolved by then, I guess I'll have to take my chances, won't I?" She raised her eyebrow, casting a disparaging glare at everyone in the room, ignoring the look of pride and adoration on Tom's face.

"A bodyguard will be with you for however long you feel is necessary." Damien stated confidently.

"No offence, but that doesn't guarantee me anything. I've never told anyone about that night but I guess today's the day, right?"

"December, you don't have to do this." Tom pleaded softly, reaching out from his seat to grasp her hands. No longer its usual soft warmness, they were cold and clammy. Her finger tips were practically icicles and he could bet blood was pounding in her ears. She gratefully squeezed his hand but she shook her head in refusal.

"I know it seems like I can't defend myself but I lived in an orphanage as a scrawny little girl with a big puff ball of hair. I could never fit in because I didn't know who I was, but I did learn how to fight for myself when it counted and I've had to do that before and I'll do it again. When Darren Singh showed up in my hotel room four years ago and held a knife to my throat, I thought I was going to die." December shut her eyes as she let herself remember that faithful night.

"I didn't even get a chance to move before he was lying on top of me, whispering and whispering. Telling me things that I'd done to anger him, to make him have to come to punish me." A sole tear trickled down her face as she recounted what happened to her. Even with her eyes closed she looked shaken.

"I tried to talk to him but it only made him more irrational to the point that he started choking me and cursing me. Which was actually a good thing, I guess since he let his knife drop on the bed and I grabbed it. I stabbed him in the shoulder and he punched me in the face. Then, he rolled off me because he was in pain and bleeding everywhere, so I crawled out of bed to the phone." December's free hand reached out to the ghost of the phone.

"I was going to call for help. I nearly had it but he was on me again. He had that damn knife again. Slashing and slashing at my pyjamas, then he started kicking me. Over and over and over..."

Every person in the room was riveted, staring mournfully as December continued, wishing it would end. Clarissa gripped Peter's arm tightly as he stood next to her, as if it were a life line.

"He dragged me up by my hair. I had it in this ridiculous bun to sleep in, you know? And he just yanked it until I struggled to my feet but I grabbed something on the way up. I hoped it was something pointy but it was my frigging blanket. I just flung it at him and got away. I picked up the lamp and hit him in the face with it, but he wouldn't go down. So I kicked him in the privates and beat him with the base of the lamp until I was so tired that I could barely pick my hand up again. Apparently I was screaming while doing that which alerted security who burst through the door and there you have it, the worst night of my life. Any questions?" She finished with a tight, bitter smile.

"I'm sorry I ever wondered, to be honest." Damien said, with no trace of humor this time.

"I told you all that so you know why I'm scared. Why I'm counting on you. I am terrified what at what this man might do to me if he gets his hands on me again. Please, please, please find him." December implored, finally allowing the tears to flow freely.

She felt deflated after letting down her guard completely, and in front of strangers, after holding on to that secret for so many years. She felt Tom wrap his arm around her shoulders, kissing the side of her head.

"Come on, sweetheart, I think you've had enough of this for now. You need some rest." He whispered, leading her back to the sanctuary of their bedroom.

Tom didn't have a clue how to console her. He felt overwhelmed, and he was devastated that December had gone through all of that alone. And for her to have to relive it? He wanted to throttle someone, preferably Darren Singh.

Chapter Nine

A visibly distressed Clarissa fled to the kitchen, with Peter following closely behind her. She wiped her eyes harshly with the back of her hand, leaving her make up smeared as she took a moment to collect herself. Judging by her reaction, he figured that this was the first time she'd heard the full story. He'd only read the details himself a few hours back but nothing ever felt real until you dealt with the victims of assault cases.

.''You okay?"

"It is a lot to take in. My mind is still reeling from everything I just learned. It just explains so much." Her eyes filled with unshed tears, causing her to look away. All Peter wanted to do right then was to kiss her.

It made him feel guilty as hell. A woman whom he admired just told him the worst news of her life, and he was standing there ogling her best friend.

This is why he didn't make eye contact with women he found attractive when he had no business being attracted to them. It made him seem like a giant jerk, but at least no one could ever accuse him of sexual harassment. Clarissa's sniffling took him out of his thoughts.

"Hey, don't cry. We're all in this together now. There wasn't a person in this room who would even dream of letting the lovely December Brown down in her time of need." Peter rested his hand gently on her shoulder to convey in sincerity, never expecting Clarissa to turn into his chest, resting her face against the crook of his neck. Peter's body automatically reacted to her, his arms encircling her waist without hesitation. He inhaled the floral fragrance of her hair shamelessly.

"I'm screwed." thought Peter as Clarissa nuzzled against him. There was no use fighting his growing attraction to her.

Clarissa didn't know why she sought comfort in Peter's arms, but it felt right. Maybe it was how rock steady he'd been throughout these past few hours, but even his woodsy scented cologne seemed to soothe her, making her feel safe and secure.

His strong, sturdy body felt amazing as she pressed up against him. She looked up into his smoke colored eyes and slid her hand into his thick, shaggy hair, pulling his head down slightly before capturing his lips in a heady, toe curling kiss.

"I need a drink after hearing that. Anybody want anything?" Damien's voice rang out as he came towards the kitchen.

They jumped apart as he rounded the corner into the room, Clarissa making her way to the furthest part of the room, somewhere between the dishwasher and stove.

"Everything okay in here?" Damien wondered, looking from a wild eyed Clarissa to a softly panting Peter. He only needed one guess to figure out what he'd just bumbled in to, so he quickly grabbed an apple and sped out of there.

"I am so sorry about that. I don't know what came over me." She blushed, feeling suddenly shy. Her fingers fluttered to her mouth where her lips still tingled from their kiss. He looked even more shocked than she felt.

"Talk about an inappropriate time to rub up on a dude," Clarissa thought to herself. She could still taste him, a mint and coffee mixture that could become very addictive if given the chance.

"Seriously, I apologize. I don't normally go around making out with strange men. Let's just pretend like that never happened. It won't end well. I don't really do the whole commitment thing, so you know, can we just forget it?" She asked, in a hushed tone.

"A kiss like that? No way!" Peter retorted, still looking awestruck, advancing upon her.

Clarissa was torn between backing up and giving in just so she could feel that electrifying feeling again. She could already tell that Peter would be a problem. He wasn't like the others. He was her fear of committed relationships embodied into one man who probably looked really good topless. She tried to shake those fuzzy feelings out of herself. Kissing him was a mistake.

She was a huge romantic when it came to everybody else, but she just didn't do the mushy stuff personally. It wasn't like she had no interest in guys or dating, but it was just too much trouble. Romance in general was too much trouble. First, it was the uncertainty, then the short lived euphoria, then the next thing you know, you're trying to figure out which family you were going to be spending Thanksgiving with while your families stress you out about it and then somewhere along the way you can't live without them but you want to push them out of the window some days. It just seemed like a lot of hassle to her.

Besides, she had her apartment just the way she wanted it and she didn't have to compromise with some guy who didn't even know what a good thread count was. Clarissa side-eyed Peter, his eyes still darkened with lust, and she sighed deeply. Yup, he probably had lots of opinions about things that didn't concern him. Like how much to spend on their daughter's birthday party.

"Oh my God, I'm losing it." She said out loud, abruptly grabbing her coat and her phone. She had to get out of there. She barely knew the guy and already she was imagining having children with him, and arguing about it. It was all too much for her.

"Hey, where are you going?" Peter called after her.

"I need to get coffee or cigarettes or scotch. I'll be right back." Clarissa yelled back, slamming the front door behind her.

Chapter Ten

The week flew by without incident. Darren hadn't surfaced. It was as if he'd disappeared without a trace after that night. There were no sightings of him in New Jersey or in New York, which Peter attributed it to him realizing that the police were after him for violating his parole.

Peter kept in touch with Clarissa via daily phone calls but she refused to meet up with him. Perhaps it was his weak excuses as to why she should meet him for coffee, or the fact that she just couldn't face him now that she'd realized that she must have looked like a fool running away like that. Either way, she didn't want to chance it.

Unfortunately, fate had a way of imposing its will on its intended targets.

"Terrence, please come! I'll even buy yours!" Clarissa begged over the phone.

"Girl, bye. I'm not coming all the way to the West Side just to go grocery shopping with you. You're not interesting and I still don't forgive you for that haircut comment." Terrence replied snarkily.

He didn't bother telling her that he was literally in Central Park walking his dog with his boyfriend, David. He had no plans to cut his day short just to go to Agatha and Valentina. That was her and December's thing.

He knew Clarissa hated food shopping alone; she basically told him that every other month. It all came down to the fact that she was the oldest of five children and grocery shopping with that many children would ruin any one's love of supermarkets. Chasing after her younger brothers and sisters was a nightmare that she'd never quite gotten over.

"I'll give you a raise." She pleaded, hoping against hope that he would take pity on her. He didn't.

"Nope. Bye. Love you." Terrence countered, hanging up quickly.

"I wasn't going to give you a raise anyway. Blah." She sassed to nobody in particular. Clarissa sighed loudly and headed out of her apartment building, barely rounding the corner before nearly bumping into someone.

"Clarissa, hi." Peter said, smiling widely.

Butterflies attacked her tummy in full force. Damn.

"Oh hey, Peter."

She hoped her reply sounded as cool and nonchalant as she hoped, instead of awkward and distant. He looked her up and down slowly, taking his time as he enjoyed the view.

"Alright, buddy, take it down a notch. Sheesh." she muttered, hotly. Ignoring the blush that was creeping from her hairline down to her cheeks, she attempted to regard him sternly.

"Sorry, I was going for a sensuous, hungry look like in those romance novels." Peter confessed, smiling the smile of the unrepentant. Clarissa laughed in spite of herself.

"You're nothing like I thought, you know? Now I find out you read erotica and you're shameless about it. I kind of like that in a man."

"I would have admitted it earlier if I knew you were into it. But I have to admit that I only read the fluffy stuff. Blame Diana for that." His steel gray eyes sparkled as he gazed at her, making her feel giddy and warm all over.

"Diana, your goddaughter, right?"

"You remembered that?" Peter asked in awe.

"Of course. I have a perfect memory. So keep that in mind if you insist on wooing me." Clarissa answered with a wink. Peter chuckled, enjoying her smile when she was mostly worry free.

"So where are you off to on this cold February day?"

"Grocery shopping. Do you live around here? Or are you on duty?"

"Today's my day off. And yeah, I live up the block. I guess we're neighbors, huh?"

"I guess so. Well, nice seeing you again. You look good. I mean, why did I say that? Oh God, I meant to say 'have a nice day'." She sputtered, red faced.

"I can take a compliment. You look great yourself. Mind if I join you? I need to get some cheese and socks." Peter said, stuffing his hands into his coat pocket

"Yeah, you don't buy socks in Agatha and Valentina but I'd love it if you'd join me. I hate shopping alone."

"Me too. I guess it's because I'm from a big family. I'm the middle child out of seven."

"Figures." Clarissa grumbled, shaking her head in defeat. Was it too much to ask for him to be an only child with estranged parents who lived in Alaska?

The closer the time came to go back to the city, December grew more and more anxious. She missed her home but couldn't shake the feeling of foreboding.

Meanwhile, Clarissa couldn't wait for her return. She was uncharacteristically excited about a guy. December desperately hoped it was Peter.

Clarissa wanted to tell her all about it over dinner in China Town later that evening. Apparently, she'd been having an amazing couple of dates with said guy, which included shopping and a long dinner where she laughed until her jaw hurt.

"I think it's Peter. If it isn't Peter, I'm going to be so mad. I wanted to play cupid for them but then I had to go and be all traumatized and flee the city with a handsome British guy." December lamented as she laid in bed with Tom, trailing her fingers up and down his flat, muscular stomach. She felt it go up and down as laughter rippled through him.

"That sounds like any James Bond movie ever."

"Doesn't it? Anyway, I'm happy that she's happy. I just think Peter would be perfect for her. She actually cared when she thought he ignored her. She nearly had a cat fight with Terrence over it, actually."

"I wish I could have seen that. I bet it was hilarious."

"I was too busy trying to stop him from snipping her bald to find the humor in it."

"Tape it next time for posterity. But as you were saying before, they'd be good together. He obviously likes her. I mean, he's going out of his way to help you. I know he's a good cop and would do a hundred percent on whatever case he worked on, but I think he's going above and beyond." Tom remarked, twirling December's hair while he spoke.

Laying in bed with her, cuddling, and talking was his favorite part of the day. She caught him up to speed with all the gossip and news when he was out of town, and she listened patiently as he ranted about this director or that producer. Even if she didn't know who it was, she never failed to make him feel as if what he was saying was insanely entertaining.

If anyone had told him a year ago that he'd be madly in love with a singer who made him laugh all the time, he'd have thought they were talking to the wrong person. Now he couldn't imagine his life without her.

"I think we should get married." Tom mused out loud. He anxiously waited for her response but she remained silent.

"December? What do you think?"

"Huh? What? I must have drifted off. You stopped talking for ages. I'm sorry. Repeat what you said?" She replied, sleepily.

"Never mind. We'll talk about it later." Tom answered quietly.

He was almost relieved that she hadn't heard his question; he didn't even have a ring picked out. She deserved more than an impromptu, half thought out proposal. Tom grinned at the ceiling of the hotel they were staying at as he mentally planned out how he was going to pop the question.

Chapter Eleven

"Clarissa, it's Pete. Sorry, I'm calling from work. I have some news. There's a man fitting Darren's description that was just hauled into the 40h Precinct, which just so happens to be in the Bronx. He didn't have any ID on him, so I'm going to go check it out. I'll let you know what happens. I'm sorry I can't make it for lunch, but I know you'll understand. Talk to you soon."

She replayed the message several times in excitement before calling Damien to let him know.

"I hope it's him. That would be a great 'welcome back' present for her." Clarissa exclaimed, dancing around her dining room.

"I know. I wouldn't tell her anything just yet until you get confirmation from your little boyfriend." Damien teased while he patiently pumped gas into his SUV. He couldn't wait until this nightmare was over so things could go back to normal. Chasing after Darren kept him away from his wife and daughter for more time than he liked.

"Everyone's little when you're a giant, Paul Bunyon. I promise I'll wait to tell her. Darius left about five minutes ago, but he told December and Tom to stay in their room until you get there. He feels bad that he wasn't able to drop them back home, but there's a family emergency, and he's only a half an hour away from where he needs to be."

"It's no problem. I'm nearly there. I've driven further for less. I'm leaving to pick them up now. We'll see you in a few hours, Blondie."

"Maurice, I need a huge favor." Tom nervously paced up and down the lobby of the Four Seasons. It was always best to be upfront and succinct with his manager, Maurice Doyle. If he tired of listening to you, he'd hang up without even a warning.

"What do you need?" Maurice sounded gruff and impatient, even on Christmas. Even his sincere Thanks sounded begrudging, but Tom didn't take it personally since Maurice was always good to him and that's what counted at the end of the day.

"I'm going to propose to December. I need the perfect ring. Can you arrange for me to go ring shopping at Tiffany's without being seen? I don't want her to find out in the news before I have the chance to ask her myself."

"You're getting married?"

"If she'll have me, of course." Tom laughed. "Are you alright, Maurice? You sounded a bit odd there."

"Never better. Just a little choked up, is all. Don't worry, we're going to find her the perfect ring."

"Why, Maurice, I didn't know you were into the lovey-dovey stuff." If he didn't know better, Tom could almost swear there was a smile in his grumpy manager's voice.

"Huge fan of it. I'll take care of everything. Talk soon." Maurice instructed and hung up. Even his abrupt hang up didn't faze Tom. He was over the moon and he hadn't even asked her yet.

"Hey babe, where were you? Damien called and said he was on his way to pick us up." December called out from the shower when he entered their hotel suite.

"I was on the phone to Maurice. Last minute arrangements and all that." Tom replied as he made his way to bathroom. He peeked in the shower and she shrieked out a giggle.

"Perv!" She flung perfumed suds of soap at him until he was forced to retreat, laughing all the way.

"How long away is he, then?" Tom asked as he unbuttoned his white dress shirt.

"He said about three-ish. So maybe thirty minutes?"

"Good. I have time for a shower." He said, surprising her by sliding into the steaming shower behind her. December's fit of helpless giggles that followed was like music to his ears.

"I don't want to go back. I can't. Not yet, anyway. He's still out there lurking, Tom. I just can't." December pleaded as overwhelming feelings of panic flooded through her veins.

Her heart rate tripled the second she spotted Damien's parked car. He waved at her but she didn't wave back. She just looked at him with wide, frantic eyes. A half an hour later and all her euphoria had vanished in a sea of frightened uncertainty.

"Sweetheart, just take a deep breath. You know we've been planning this. Damien is blocking up traffic as we speak. It'll be fine, okay? Darren hasn't been seen in a week. He probably crawled back under whatever rock he emerged from in the first place." Tom soothed, rubbing her arms to calm her down.

"I don't feel good. My stomach hurts. I just want to go back upstairs into our suite and hide out for a few more days. I promise I'll be ready then. Promise." She wasn't pretending. She felt awful and scared. The feelings of dread were back in full force.

"We're not going back home, remember? We're going to meet Clarissa at your favorite restaurant in China Town. Then we're going to bunk in Clarissa's spare room where you will stay for a few days before heading off to do your music video, and then you're flying to luxurious Santa Barbara to do that charity event for Transgendered Teenagers. After that, it's Valentine's Day and we'll be together again. I have something amazing planned, too."

"Where will we be then?" December asked in a small voice.

"Miami."

It was the farthest place in the US that Tom could quickly think of that she'd want to be in on Valentine's Day, but it seemed to please her, so now he supposed they were going to Miami.

"I'm going to sit in the back seat. I still don't feel so good, so hopefully I'll fall asleep."

"That's a good idea. It's a long ride. Maybe it'll help settle your nerves." Tom added, as he held the car door open for her.

"Hey, Clarissa." Despite the fact it was a professional call, being able to talk to her still made his day.

"Peter, hi. Any good news?" She asked hopefully.

"No, I'm sorry. It wasn't him. But no news is still good news, right?"

"I doubt December will see it that way. At least she'll be here with me. Worst comes to worst, she'll go home to Philadelphia until it's time for her to get back to work."

"Yeah, that'll keep her busy. Anyway, I'll be back in Manhattan in about an hour. Back to work."

"I missed seeing you today." Clarissa blurted out, impulsively. She wanted to sink into the ground in embarrassment the instant the words came out of her mouth. It was too soon to say stuff like that, wasn't it?

"I missed you too. I can't wait to see you again. Maybe tomorrow night?" Peter responded without hesitation, grinning ear to ear.

"Only if you want to hang out at my place. We can make home-made pizza and watch one of Tom's movies while December sobs quietly into the popcorn. It's a thing she does... don't ask."

"That actually sounds amazing and I'll probably film it and put it on YouTube." Peter said, snickering at the image that popped into his head.

"Ha ha. Anyway, let me know if anything changes on the Darren Singh front."

"I will. Talk soon."

Clarissa made sure the call ended before jumping up and down in joy. She danced all the way to her closet to pick her clothes out for later that night.

Chapter Twelve

"Peter? What are you doing here?" She poked her head out into the hallway of her apartment building.

When she'd answered the door, she expected to see Tom and December standing before her but instead, it was Peter with a gloomy expression on his handsome face.

"I'm sorry, Clarissa, but I figured you'd rather hear it from me than some stranger." He replied, in a strange, pained way.

"Sorry about what? What are you talking about?"

Her heart rate sped up at the implications his words meant sped through her mind. Instantly, she went into denial mode; however, Peter insisted on trying to drag her back to reality, kicking and screaming.

"Clarissa, I'm here about December. There's been an accident."

"What? What are you saying?"

"Damien was driving when it happened. He's the one that called me. I don't know all the particulars but they're at Lenox Hill Hospital. I'll take you. You shouldn't be driv-."

Peter moved towards her, ready to console her but she pivoted out of his way. She didn't want to be consoled. She wanted Darren to go away forever and for Peter to stop looking at her like that. It was enough to send any person into hysterics.

"I need...I need you to stop talking for like ten seconds because I think I'm hallucinating."

"Clarissa, please just listen." Peter reached out to her again, but from her tense body language, he realized she didn't want to held, so he let his arms drop to his sides and backed off.

"No, be quiet! You told me to have faith and to trust you. You said you'd be able to help me keep them safe, and all of a sudden there's a car accident? No! I don't want to hear any more!" Clarissa paced back and forth in front of him, holding a hand to her chest as if she was forcing her heart to stay in there by sheer force of will.

"I'm sorry."

"You're sorry? Really? You're sorry? I'm the sorry one for ever believing you in the first place. Who are you, anyway? You're just some guy who happens to wear a badge." She hissed with a bone-chilling fury. Peter flinched as Clarissa continued to glare at him as she grabbed her coat and handbag.

"If you're here to take me to the hospital, you aren't doing a bang up job at that, either." she added coldly, breezing past him out the door.

Peter stood frozen in her apartment. Hurt, guilt, and anger welled up inside him. He took a couple of deep breaths to try and get back into a calm place before having to deal with her again. He knew she only lashed out because she was upset and afraid but he was only human and her words wounded him in a way not many ever had.

After a minute, but what felt like ages, he gripped the door knob and shut it firmly behind him, making his way out of Clarissa's building. He caught sight of her lemon blonde hair as she climbed into a yellow taxi.

"Clarissa! Wait!" he yelled, running to the curb, but he was too late. The cab sped off down the street.

Peter hurriedly walked to his double parked car and unlocked it. He knew where she was headed and like it or not, he had a job to do. Clarissa was just going to have to accept his help.

Clarissa flew through the hospital hallways towards the waiting area that the nurse pointed her to. She spotted Damien instantly. His surfer blonde hair was a tangled mess. He had stitches above his eyebrow and a nasty looking bruise on his face.

"Oh Damien, look at you," she said sorrowfully. Her eyes were wild and weary.

"Hey, hey...come here. Come on, take a deep breath." He said wrapping his arms around her shoulder. She did as she was told, but couldn't relax any more than that. She pulled away to assess him.

"Are you okay? What happened? How are they? Where's December? I don't see December?" Clarissa rushed out, looking frantically around. Damien stopped her with a steady hand on her shoulder. He glanced up in time to see Peter approaching them.

"Hey, Peter, glad you got her here so fast. Thanks, man."

Clarissa spun around to face him when she heard his name. Rage and blame colored her face but she didn't correct her friend's assumption. Instead, she just stared at him with fire in her dark green eyes. His gaze never wavered from hers. Damien, noticing the tension, cleared his throat and answered Clarissa's questions, bringing the focus back to the crisis at hand.

"We were on our way back to their place. I was driving, Tom was in the passenger seat talking to me while December took a nap in the back seat. Out of nowhere, this car just rear-ended us. It wasn't a fender bender or anything. There was definite purpose when it smashed into the back of my Range Rover. I swear, it was at least twice. I crashed into a light post."

"Oh my God," Clarissa gasped.

"Did you see who was driving?" Peter asked, putting his arm around Clarissa briefly before realizing what he'd done.

"No, but I saw the car. I couldn't miss it if I tried, it was a Hummer. I think I saw some of the plate. Not all bu..."

"Where are December and Tom?" she broke in, not caring about car makes or models right now. Not when Damien hadn't told them the important part.

"Sorry, I wanted to give you a moment, you know? You looked like you were at the end of your rope when you came in." he explained, sheepishly.

"Okay, but now I'm calm so just tell me"

"Tom broke some ribs but he'll be fine. He's in with the doctor right now"

"Oh, thank God. And December? Is she in there with him?"

He shook his head sadly. Pinpricks of tears made her eye twitch but she refused to give in.

"Damien, I swear if you don't tell me..."

"They think it's a bleed on her brain from head trauma. She's in surgery. Sh... she didn't wake up no matter how hard I tried. The doctors kept saying critical... " He rushed out through trembling lips. A pained cry escaped from Clarissa as her legs crumpled beneath her. Peter caught her in time before she hit the floor.

"Clarissa, I'm sorry." Damien piteously cried out, his head in his hands as she sobbed loudly into Peter's chest.

Chapter Thirteen

"She's in surgery. The doctors are going to help her. You can't give up on her when you don't know the outcome of the surgery. Just hang on." Peter explained into her hair as he rocked her in his arms. He went on like this for ages, being the rational, logical voice that kept trying to throw her a lifeline in her despair. When she finally felt like she couldn't cry anymore, reason started to seep in. Once she got to see December, Clarissa would know. She would know how to handle things, how to fix things, where to go from here. At least that's what her intuition was telling her.

"I need to speak to a doctor or a nurse to know how long that surgery will be," she said, sitting up and wiping her eyes. Peter handed her his handkerchief. She furrowed her brows in confusion for a moment.

"Who carries a hankie still? Are you from the 1800's?" she asked, her voice sounding watery and weird. She needed to blow her nose but didn't want to do it in front of Peter.

"Do you not want it?"

"Yes, I do. Thank you. You're still an old timey detective, though. Where's Damien?"

"Right here." he said in a small voice. He was six foot, seven inches of hunky muscle and yet at that moment he sounded like someone who needed a cuddle very badly. Clarissa made her way over to where he sat, pulling him into a tight hug.

"I'm sorry. She's going to be fine. I just know it," she said as she threaded her fingers through his hair. He rested his head against her chest with his arms wrapped around her waist.

"I think it was Darren behind the wheel of that car, Clarissa. It's a gut feeling."

"I think so, too. So we can't let him get away with hurting our family right?"

"Right."

"Let's help Peter do his job. I'll call Terrence and Maurice. Have you already called Marilyn?"

"Yeah, I told her not to come. Not yet, anyway."

"Alright, good. Well, let's do what we do best. Call your team and get them to meet us here."

"Done.," he said, already sounding like his normal self. He unfolded himself out of the chair, already whipping out his cell phone.

Clarissa rubbed her face roughly, taking away what little makeup was left after her flood of tears. She knew she looked like a mess with a bright red, slightly runny, nose and puffy eyes. She would worry about that later. Exhaling loudly, she turned to Peter who sat watching her with an unfathomable look on his face.

"What?"

"Nothing. You're just...my kind of woman." He admitted, shocking himself. Clarissa's lip quirked into a smile.

"There you go again, talking like you're from the 40's. You're Colombo reincarnated." she joked.

"Probably. What do you need me to do?"

"I like a man who knows how to take orders." He grinned at her. She smiled back before the gravity of the situation hit her all over again.

"Peter, we think it was Darren who did this."

"So do I. I heard some of what you said. If we work together, I'm sure we can end this. I have the might of the NYPD behind me."

"Peter, I just want to apologize for how I spoke to you earlier. I was out of line and I'm sorry."

"I get it. You were angry and frustrated for an actually valid reason. It's okay. Besides, in my line of work, I'm used to getting abuse."

"Thanks for understanding. Seriously." Clarissa kissed him lightly on the cheek as she walked towards lobby to make her phone calls.

"Maurice? It's Clarissa."

"Yeah, I know. Your name comes up when you call." he responded in his abrupt way. Maurice was not a fan of idle chit chat, no matter how much he liked you. Therefore, when you talked to him on the phone, you either adopted that same manner or you would end up talking to air when he hung up on you the second he figured out what you wanted from him.

"Sorry. Force of habit. Listen, I'm going to need your help because I don't think I'm in the right frame of mind right now."

"What do you need?"

"Tom and December were in a car accident earlier. Tom will be fine, just a few broken ribs as far as I know..." She waited to let Maurice absorb the news. She knew how much he cared about Tom and she refused to overlook his feelings.

"He's okay?" He audibly sighed with relief.

"Yeah, he's going to be fine."

"What happened?"

"We think it was December's stalker."

"Wow. How is she?"

"In a bad way, Maurice. She's in critical condition and still in surgery. I haven't heard anything from the doctors yet."

"Damn. I'm sorry."

"Me too. I need you to handle the press for me. I need to handle things here. Can you do that for me?"

"Got it. Which hospital?"

"Lenox Hill. Neurosurgery department. Tom's in Radiology."

"Got it. Go take care of our girl. I don't think Tom would ever get over losing her. I'll handle things on my end."

"Thanks so much, Maurice. I'll keep you updated."

"Good." The sudden silence let Clarissa know that he'd ended the call.

"Why can't he just say bye like a normal human being?" she muttered, peeking around the corner in case a doctor appeared in the hallway. However, no one appeared so she had to bite the bullet and call Terrence. It would be harder to stay tear free with him, but he would also be a great source of comfort and support. Also, he would personally strangle her if he found this out in the news, which was going to happen sooner than later.

"Hey, girl what's up?" Terrence answered, cheerfully.

"Where are you right now?"

"I was just about to hop in the shower. Why?"

"Terry, there's been an accident. December's in critical condition. I haven't seen hide nor hair of a doctor or a nurse that's dealing with either of them."

"Oh, Jesus. Baby girl." Terrence gasped, his mind flashed with images of her.

"I know. I can barely stop shaking." Clarissa confessed.

"What happened? How's Tom? Was anyone else hurt?" He was already slipping his shoes on.

"Tom's got some broken ribs, apparently. Damien is fine, just some stitches. We think it was Darren. Peter is checking in to that. Can you come to the hospital?"

"Of course, I'm on my way. Do you need me to get anything? Bring anything?"

"I just need you, Terr. Thanks, babe. See you soon?"

"Definitely. Love you!"

"Love you too, bye."

Chapter Fourteen

"The press is going crazy over the crash. Every channel has it on loop as 'Breaking News'. It's a mad house outside the hospital. I'm going to pull all the guys I can get out there to keep some order." Peter announced striding in to the waiting area.

"Ugh, I can't think about that right now. I haven't been able to get in touch yet with December's adoptive mother but at least I've spoken to spoken to the Chief of Medicine and got her permission to move Tom and December into a private room together. I convinced her it would be less taxing on her hospital staff and security that way. And yet I still haven't spoken to the doctors who are operating on her. No one has told me anything!" Clarissa exclaimed, pacing back and forth.

Peter caught her arm, forcing her to pause in her steps.

"December's being looked after. There's nothing you can do for her but be patient. Why don't you go check on Tom? He needs someone in there with him."

Clarissa smiled gratefully at him. "You're right. Thank you. I'll text the others to let them know where the private wing is so they can just meet there. If there's any problem, call me and I'll be back here like a shot." she closed the space between them, kissing him lightly before speeding off in search of the Radiology ward.

"We were just about to move him. Great timing, he seems a little distressed." A tall male nurse explained, moving aside slightly to reveal an agitated Tom, who looked worse for wear.

"How is he?"

"Two fractured ribs, sprained ankle, and a couple of bruises. Nothing a strong guy like himself can't handle" He replied, grinning at Tom who offered a small half smile. His face looked pasty and grayish from his own trauma.

"Can we have a moment, please?" Clarissa asked quietly.

"Sure. I'll just get his belongings in order."

"Tom..." She rushed to his side and hugged him gingerly. "How're you feeling?"

"I'll survive. Where's December?" His eyes flickered to the doorway. A stricken expression set in when she didn't magically appear.

"She's in surgery still, Tom. Don't worry though because I've arranged for you two to share a room in the private wing. You'll see her as soon as she's out." Clarissa squeezed his hand reassuringly. His lips flattened out into grim line as he clenched his jaw.

"Was it Darren who did this?"

"That's not it import-"

"Was it him? Was it?" He interrupted, becoming increasingly distressed with each word. He repeatedly dragged a trembling hand through his short dark hair.

"We think so, yes. Damien and Peter aren't going to rest until they get him. I swear to you, he'll never hurt either of you again." Clarissa pledged.

Utter anguish flooded his face, making his eyes red and watery as he struggled with the flood of emotion. He looked away, rapidly blinking to keep the tears at bay but a few escaped nonetheless.

"She knew this would happen. I convinced her to get in the car when she didn't want to. She knew something like this would happen. Clarissa, she begged me not to make her come back and I didn't listen and now...Oh God. Please don't let her die." he pleaded, choking back a sob. Clarissa stood frozen. She couldn't think of what to say to help ease his mind when she felt the same way.

The nurse appeared, casting a concerned glance from Tom to Clarissa.

"I think you need to get some rest, Mr. Elmswood. It'll do you good."

Clarissa read his name tag, Gabriel Ruiz, RN., and committed it to memory. He deserved a raise but since she didn't have the authority, at least she could send him some concert or even movie premiere tickets.

She mouthed "Thanks" as he administered a sedative to help Tom sleep.

""Where's Maurice? I have to call Sister Florence, she needs to be here." Tom wondered as Nurse Ruiz helped him get into a more comfortable position on his hospital bed.

"I've spoken to Maurice, he's on his way. So is Terrence and no one is answering at the church. But I'll keep calling until I get her, okay? When you wake up, you'll be in your new room."

"That's good. Please get in touch with my mother or else she'll be worried and I won't hear the end of it." Tom said sleepily, barely able to keep his eyes opened.

"She adores December. Everyone does. Not as much as me though."

"No, not as much as you." Clarissa agreed with a sorrowful smile.

"I brought you a latte. Any news?" Terrence leaned down to kiss her on the cheek and handed her the hot drink before taking the uncomfortable seat next to her.

"Ooh, thank you, this is just what I needed. Well, she's out of surgery, so hopefully the doctor will be out soon to talk us and then we can see her. Tom's still out though, thank goodness." Clarissa answered, massaging the bridge of her nose in exhaustion.

"I can't believe this happened. I'm still in shock. Dee barely has to go to the doctor and now she just had surgery to stop bleeding on her brain?"

"I know." They sat quietly, staring at the cold white walls in front of them.

"You know she'll milk this for all its worth, don't you?"

Clarissa snorted despite being teary eyed.

"I know. Every time we tell her no, she'll bring it up."

He smiled sadly, nodding. Once again, silence invited itself to the conversation as they sat sipping their drinks. After a while Terrence spoke again, his voice sounding wobbly.

"She'll be fine, right?"

"Of course she will. She has to be." Clarissa laid her head on his shoulder. It was eating her up inside having to reassure everyone else when she longed for it herself.

"Where's Tom's manager? I thought he'd be here by now?"

"He's handling everything media related but he's on his way."

"Oh, okay."

"Speaking of which, how was it out there? Peter said there were some NYPD officers outside keeping order?" Clarissa asked, wrapping both hands around the cup of steaming liquid, enjoying the heat emanating from within.

"Some? He should have said nearly all! It's literally pure insanity out there. I barely shoved my way in so I can only imagine how bad it will be later on. Her fans are pouring in from all over the city and Tom's too. It's crazy."

"Can you call David and ask him to record as much footage as he can? I bet they would love to see all this outpouring of love for them." She suggested. Terrence perked up instantly.

"Oh, that's a great idea. I'll call him now."

"I'm going to go hover around the door to their room. Maybe her doctors will take the hint and come outside faster. This waiting thing is killing me." Clarissa shouted after him as he headed further down the hallway for privacy.

Chapter Fifteen

Tom kept his breathing steady while pretending to sleep until the doctors and nurses exited the room. It took everything he had not to jump out of his hospital bed the moment he saw December being wheeled in, but he knew they would try and stop him.

From his position he could see the side of her face as she laid flat in the bed opposite his. He listened to her breathing through her oxygen mask and the beeping sounds of the heart rate and blood pressure monitors.

Tom took a deep, painful breath and forced himself into a sitting position. He could see her eyes were closed now, with several intravenous drips connected to her arm. Tom groaned when he put pressure on his sprained ankle but it wasn't enough to slow him down as he hobbled to December's bedside.

He stared down at her unconscious face framed by a cloud of honey-brown hair; her pupils moved rapidly as she dreamt. He caressed her cheek and slowly sat down at the side of the bed.

"Sweetheart, I'm so sorry. I should have listened to you. We should still be in that hotel room snuggled up, ordering room service. We could still do that, in fact. On Valentine's Day, we could be locked away all safe and sound in a hotel room, binge watching The Mindy Project...doesn't that sounds great? If you open your eyes right now, I'll even watch that Cinderella movie with Whitney Houston in it that you love so much. Just open your eyes, my love. Or squeeze my hand...please." He took her small hands in his and brought it to his lips.

Tom punctuated each tender kiss of her hand with a mournful 'please' until his mouth ran dry and his eyes burned from crying.

Finally, Tom shifted on her bed until he lay down beside her, grateful for the painkillers that made moving around somewhat bearable. He gently pecked her cheek.

"Marry me, December. Wake up, say yes, and marry me. Make me the happiest man in the universe. We can go to Tiffany's and pick out a ring. Any ring you want." Tom whispered against her temple.

The heart rate monitor's beeping sped up, much faster than the steady rhythm Tom had grown used to. He panicked as December's body began to thrash about. He quickly started pressing the call button for the nurse's station, and bellowed for help

"You scared me the life out of me. Look, I have several gray hairs now because of you." Tom complained, all the while covering her face in kisses.

"Well, I didn't know I had a feeding tube down my throat." December rasped, her throat still raw.

They had found out the hard way that regaining consciousness was very dramatic when you had something lodged in your esophagus. Nothing was more frightening than seeing a loved one's body convulsing and feeling completely helpless, which was how Tom felt, when he was pushed out of the way when the doctors and nurses burst through the hospital room doors. They were followed closely by a frazzled Clarissa, Peter, and Terrence. After five excruciating minutes where medical staff surrounded December and nobody told them anything, they were given the news they all desperately wanted to hear.

"She's awake. We're still monitoring her but I don't see why she won't make a full recovery if there aren't any complications."

The entire room erupted with relieved cheers before they were ushered out to let the patients sleep. Tom stayed glued to December's side, regardless of what the doctors and nurses advised him to do, which ended with them relenting and there he remained.

Hours later when she woke up officially, he still held her, eager to have groggy, scratchy throat conversations with her.

"Could you hear me when you unconscious?" Tom pondered, threading his fingers through hers. She weakly moved her head side to side. Everything hurt but it felt nice to be near one another.

"It's all a little blurry to me right now. The last thing I remember was falling asleep in the back of Damien's car. Where is he, anyway? Is he okay?"

"Yes, just a few scratches. I don't know where he is, though."

"He's probably chasing down Darren as we speak." She guessed softly. Her voice sounded hoarse and her tongue felt thick and heavy in her dry mouth.

"How do you know it was him?"

"I can feel it in my bones, Tom. I know was him." December insisted firmly.

"I'm sorry I didn't listen to your feelings before. I should have put your needs first. I was utterly selfish. Please forgive me."

"It wasn't your fault. Stop blaming yourself because a psychopath with boundary issues decided to be obsessed with trying to kill me. I'm so sorry you and Damien were dragged into this."

"I don't know what I would have done if anything had happened to you."

"A one man vendetta?"

"Definitely. Like Lex Luthor."

"There are so many things wrong with your choice." She tried to laugh but it was mostly a groan.

"What's wrong with Lex Luthor?"

"He's a villain. He's not trying to seek justice for anything."

"Yeah, but look at his suits. He's an inspiration."

"You're the worst, but I love you."

"And I love you. You're the best thing that ever happened to me, December Brown."

"Me too, baby. I'm going to shut my eyes for a few minutes, okay? Wake me when Nunny gets here, please."

"Of course, sweetheart. Do you want me to go back to my bed now?" December moaned out a no before slipping away in to a hazy dreamland.

"We got him." Peter bellowed excitedly, rushing towards Clarissa and lifting her up. She had been walking back and forth impatiently waiting for a chance to see December awake again. The first time was much too fleeting for her liking. She'd only gotten to kiss her forehead before Terrence shoved her aside for his turn.

"What?" Clarissa asked, stunned. She couldn't have heard him right.

"Clarissa, we frigging caught him. He snuck into the building dressed as a janitor but Damien recognized him before he could get anywhere." He reiterated, spinning her around in the air.

"What?" She repeated, shrilly. Disbelief and hope warred with her expressions.

"It's over, babe. He's going away for a very long time. We even have the car with his fingerprints all over it."

"It's over?"

Peter nodded, grinning like the cat that got the cream. Clarissa was speechless. Without thinking she let out an almighty shriek, then grabbed his face with both hands and kissed him. She broke away from the kiss and began to pull away.

"Oh no, not this time!" Peter exclaimed, pulling her back to him. He slipped one hand into Clarissa's hair and the other on the small of her back before kissing her so thoroughly she became boneless against him.

When they finally needed to come up for air, he brushed a few loose strands from her face, made sure she was steady on her feet, kissed her briefly once more and finally let her go.

"Alright, you can go now." he said gently pushing her with a pat on the butt, in the direction he knew she'd want to go first.

"You're going to pay for that, Peter Bassano." Clarissa vowed, stumbling away and fanning herself. Peter's arrogant laughter followed her all the way down the hall.

December sobbed with relief when Clarissa told her the news. Her grip was fierce on her best friend's hand as she thanked her for everything she did.

"It was Damien and Peter, I didn't do anything but yell at people and cry. Don't ever scare us like that again, okay?" Clarissa warned, tearfully.

"I'll try." December replied, lying propped up slightly in her hospital bed. Terrence brushed and styled her hair to hide the shaved off part from the surgery but she refused to let him put make up on her.

"My face hurts too much, and besides I look like someone took a sharpened cheese grater to half of my face with all these cuts. Isn't it great? Take pics quickly, so we can email this to everyone. Think of all the get well gifts I could get."

"See, I told you." Terrence said turning to Clarissa, shaking his head. "I'm actually judging you right now, Dee."

"But I nearly died." She pouted.

"That's too soon, December. Tom, please control your woman. She's a terrible person." Terrence lamented, but found no help from Tom or Clarissa who both thought it was a great idea.

"Tom, someone's here to see you." Peter announced, entering the room with flowers from the hospital gift store.

A short, grumpy, middle-aged man in a business suit bustled in after him. The second he saw Tom's smiling face, his mouth contorted into something that resembled a smile. It was a little disconcerting to watch but in the end, it was all for Tom, who looked very touched by the display.

"Maurice, you finally made it."

"Yeah, I had a couple of stops to make before I could get here."

Maurice strode over to Tom's side of the bed and embraced him briefly.

"Don't ever scare me like that again. Estelle sends you her love and this." He held out a tiny black velvet box where only Tom could see.

"What is it?" Tom's asked, quizzically.

"It was her mother's. Now it's yours. December, when you're up for it, we'd love it if you came over for dinner."

"I would absolutely love that, Maurice. Thank you." She answered eagerly

"Knock, knock." Trace poked his head through the door. "Geez, what a crowd in here."

"Trace! You didn't have to come, but I'm glad you did."

"Of course I'd be here. And I come bearing gifts. I found this old bag hanging around in the wrong corridor."

"Hey, watch your mouth, you little punk! " Sister Florence admonished, poking him in the back as she trailed in after him.

"Where's my sweet baby? I'm so sorry I didn't get here sooner. We were out on a field trip and I forgot to charge my phone, as usual. Ugh. Scoot out of the way, you two."

She playfully swatted Terrence and Clarissa away with her purse so she could fuss over December. They were used to being hustled around by the pint sized Asian nun, who adored the very bones of their friend.

"Hi, Sister Florence." They said in unison.

"Nunny, I'm going to be okay. They caught him." December explained between peppered kisses all over face.

"Good. Look at these horrible bruises on your pretty face." Sister Florence tutted, turning her face left and right to examine her wounds.

"It'll heal, Nunny."

"And Tommy, look at you, too. Clarissa, you didn't tell me Tommy hurt his face." She cast an accusatory glance her way.

"Well, you hung up the second I said surgery, so I didn't get a chance." Clarissa explained, holding her hands up in surrender.

Sister Florence swatted her again as she passed around the bed to get to Tom.

"Ow! I didn't even do anything." Clarissa sulked, holding her arm for Peter to see. He gave it a smooch just in case.

"Who's the grumpy young man standing in my way?"

"Nunny, it's Maurice. You met him at our New Year's Eve party, remember?" December pressed her face into Tom's shoulder, stifling a laugh. Maurice's shocked face at being called a young man at nearly sixty was priceless. He subconsciously touched his thinning gray hair and scowled.

"I had too much to drink that night, I don't remember." She whacked Maurice with her purse until he moved, just for good measure.

Which to be honest was how she met him at the party. He was hogging the dip and Sister Florence, who at age seventy-five didn't believe in waiting on lines, or saying excuse me. With a sharp tongue and kind heart, she was a favourite at parties.

"I have broken ribs and a sprained ankle, too." Tom whined, enjoying the attention as fretted over his injured features. He adored Nunny and she doted on him as much as she did December.

"Is no one going to introduce me to the handsome policeman?" Sister Florence wondered at the top of her voice, eyeing Peter up as he chatted with Trace and Terrence.

"This is Peter Bassano, Sister. He's a police detective." Clarissa answered, lacing her fingers through his.

"He's your boyfriend?"

"I wouldn't say all…"

"So that's a yes, then?" Clarissa blushed and turned to Peter, who wiggled his eyebrows at her.

"Yes, Sister Florence."

"Good taste. I like him. Tell him to bring me a chair to sit down. I'm old."

Epilogue

"Peter, can you get this last box? I don't know what you have in it but it's heavy as hell." Clarissa yelled down the stairs.

"On my way, my little turtle dove." He bounded up the stairwell of his now empty apartment. Although Peter seemed unperturbed by the impending move, Clarissa was starting to have last minute doubts.

"Are you sure you want to move in together?" She asked as he bent down.

"You ask this now when I literally have the final cardboard box filled with my weights and computer monitor in my arms? You're not getting out of this."

"Who taught you how to pack? Who puts those two items together?" Clarissa quipped, shaking her head in exasperation.

"Well we can't all be smart and beautiful, can we?" Peter gave her a peck on the cheek and disappeared down the steps.

Clarissa shook her head. There was no use trying to argue with him, he just kept sweet talking her. It wasn't that she didn't want to move in with Peter, in fact she loved Peter. Dating him was effortless but scary because falling for him was easy. Too easy in fact, and that worried her. What if she was setting herself up for failure? Sure he made her laugh, challenged her, adored her friends, got along with her family, never complained about her work schedule, and was incredibly romantic without being corny but what if one day she woke up and found that he was actually super annoying and she hated him. Or worse, what if he hated her and didn't know how to tell her? And now they were moving in together, and not into the safety of her apartment or even his, but a new one they bought together. None of those levels of commitment bothered her until extremely recently.

It all felt natural until today when they started the actual moving process. It didn't help that his seven siblings and their spouses and children all turned up along with her 5 siblings plus December, Tom, Damien, Terrence and David. It was like a traveling circus except everyone was annoying and slightly pissed off.

Maybe it was too soon.

"It's not too soon."

Clarissa looked around scared and confused. Where did that voice come from, was she going crazy?

"I think you've finally snapped. I'm in the next room, you weirdo. Stop talking to yourself and come over here. I brought you a sandwich wrap. Peter said you were up here talking to yourself. Come eat." December called out.

"Oh thank goodness. I'm starving." She sat beside December on the dark wood floor of the now vacant living room.

"Care to tell me why you are having an existential crisis out loud?" December handed her a chicken and avocado wrap and she quickly tore the paper off, eager for a bite.

"I was saying that stuff out loud? How much did you hear?"

"Well you said something about a traveling circus. Anyway so you're telling me that you went apartment shopping, went through escrow and now after all of that, you are now second guessing the decision to buy a place together?"

"It sounds pretty bad when you put it like that." She muttered through a full mouth.

"Clarissa, I love you. You're the most organized, level headed person I have ever met, but you're a big dummy if you think for an instant that moving in with Peter is the wrong decision."

"It's not?"

"You're the happiest I've ever seen you. Also you could totally buy another apartment any time you want. You're rich remember?" December reminded her, wisely as she nibbled on a salad. Her fitness instructor had her own another diet, needless to say she was not impressed.

"Okay, you have a point there but what about all those horrible family holidays? We'll be fighting every year trying to figure out which house to go to. It's going to be awful times two." Clarissa bemoaned, suddenly losing her appetite.

"Or double the presents?" December offered, quickly scooping up the rest of Clarissa's lunch.

"Spoken like a person who doesn't have to show up for those things."

"Right? And Tom's an only child too so it's extra fun." December grinned, wickedly.

"You're evil." Clarissa laughed, stabbing a fork into her friend's discarded bowl of leaves and nuts.

"Seriously though, maybe you should talk to Peter about your worries over the move. It will help." December stood up, wiping the dust off her worn out jeans.

"Let's have brunch tomorrow before you leave for Vancouver."

"Sure. We don't leave until four in the afternoon. I don't know why Tom even wants to go back on that show. I love Trace and all but I still cringe when I think about that day."

"But look how happy you are now!"

"That's true. I still don't want to go though. At least Terrence will be forced to come too. Tom wants us to dress extra glamorous...so basically I'm going to be freezing to death in front of a live studio audience. Hooray."

"You could always dress demurely." Clarissa offered, half sarcastically.

"Or wear something shiny which is what glamour means to me."

"At least you're out of your velvet phase."

"Pete, I'm home. Where are you?" Clarissa called out, locking the front door. She dropped her coat and handbag on a pile of boxes and looked around in dismay. Every time she thought about unpacking she was seized with that strong feeling of uncertainty all over again.

"Babe, I'm in the bedroom. I have a surprise for you."

"Are you naked? Because you've used that surprise like 30 times now." Clarissa made her way to their bedroom, dodging the mess they called belongings.

"No you pervert. The four poster bed we ordered arrived so I set it up. Ta-da" Peter announced, proudly, gesturing to the giant carved mahogany sleeping structure in the middle of the room.

"Oh wow! This looks fantastic! I'm so glad you did this. I was dreading having to try to build it with you." She trailed her fingers over the smooth edges in awe.

"Really? Why?" Peter asked, taken aback by her words.

"Well I anticipated the stress of doing a DIY project with you, especially since I'm horrible at that kind of stuff."

"Hmm." He scratched his soon to be bearded face. He really needed a shave or so Clarissa kept telling him.

"Hmm? What does that mean?" She folded her arms and raised her eyebrows as he waited for his response.

"You anticipated stressing out over a potential project in general or with me specifically?" Peter responded, turning to look at her expectantly. She sighed deeply.

"Honestly, all I could think of was the tug of war for control, and the inevitable seeds of resentment being sown."

"Wow. You really over thought that." Peter retorted, dryly. "Anything else you're worried about?"

"Yes. The decorating, I've aged five years just thinking about that process."

"Because of the tug of war for control and inevitable resentment?"

"Yes."

Peter sat down on the mattress, patting the space next to him. Clarissa sat down reluctantly.

"Why didn't you just talk to me about this before?" She shrugged.

Clarissa, do you remember how my apartment looked?" Peter asked patiently.

"How could I forget? I still have flashbacks of a random mural of an ape, exposed brick and a water barrel being used as a coffee table. What were you thinking?"

"I wasn't and that's the truth. Hell, I found that orange couch on the side of the street in Brooklyn."

"Ew, we made out on that." Clarissa scowled in disgust but Peter only laughed.

"Right? I don't even remember if I had it cleaned or just accepted it just the way it was. The point is, I could have gotten lice all because I am genuinely the worst."

Clarissa nodded in complete agreement.

"Anyway what I'm trying to say is that you run a successful franchise called December Brown, and I trust you completely and I would be a fool not to, because I want nothing to do with how our place looks. You want something fixed, please call me. I love that stuff, but I do not give a damn about sheet counts." Peter explained passionately.

"Thread counts" she corrected.

"Okay, thread counts or what's the difference between a comforter and a duvet cover."

"Well actually they-" Peter cut her off with a kiss.

"I don't care. I trust you, you have amazing taste. You have nothing to worry about."

"What about when we have kids and I want to have an elaborate party to celebrate their birthdays?" She ventured, feeling bold.

"Will there be cake?"

"Duh."

"Well then I'm here when you need me. I'm actually happy that you love planning everything. It makes life so much easier for me. I come home at crazy times when I'm working a case and I don't really want the hassle."

"I agree completely. After spending the day running around bossing people around, I just want to enjoy our life together for those few hours before we pass out in front of the TV."

"I'm not against hiring a cleaning lady or a handy man if it will ease the burden of doing things."

"That's the sweetest thing you've ever said to me."

"Since we're being honest, I have a major concern myself."

"Really? Okay what?" She sat back on the bed, crossing her legs. Peter exhaled loudly.

"Family holidays."

"I'm listening"

"I was thinking if we spend Christmas Eve at mine, and Christmas day at yours, we can avoid the hassle of trying to decide."

"What?" Clarissa stared at him, open mouthed.

"Well my parent's house is usually jam packed on Christmas day, you can't sit down and its exhausting, However on Christmas eve all the kids come over to bake cookies, and open gifts from the uncles and aunties. It's way more enjoyable that day." Peter clarified.

"Yes, I love this idea and I love you and yes!" Clarissa shrieked, climbing into his lap. She felt liberated by relief, all her worry lifted weightlessly off her shoulders by his unsuspecting words.

"Aww, I love you too. Are you sure? It won't be too much trouble?" He wrapped his arms around her waist, thrilled that she was so excited about his suggestion.

"No, Peter. No trouble at all." Clarissa whispered, flinging her arms around his neck in glee.

"The last time these two people were on my show, I kind of sort of embarrassed the hell out of them. Apparently they're gluttons for punishment because they're back on Trace Randall Tonight, so let's give huge round of applause for America's favorite couple, Tom Elmswood and December Brown."

Tom placed his hand on the small of her back making contact with her smooth perfumed skin due to her glittery silver, backless dress, sending shivers through her spine as they walked to the stage with thunderous applause. They smiled and waved, hugging their host once they arrived on the stage set.

"December, you look delectable in that dress. Give us a twirl"

She spun around happily, eager to show the sparkly diamond like sequinned effect the knee length fitted dress gave off when she did. The entire auditorium exploded in rapturous praise.

"Absolutely beautiful! Have a seat, my love. I want to ogle your boyfriend now." Trace instructed as he helped her to the show's familiar dark blue couch. She winced as she flashbacked to the night she first met Tom on it. No matter how hard she tried, she could not think of it as a good memory. The media didn't remember it all that positively either.

"Tom, wow! This is how you wear a suit, people. Take notes. I'm already lost in his eyes and he just got on the stage. Now ladies and gentleman, this is a gorgeous man. I'm talking he came out of the womb hot! I know, I saw the home movie." The audience hooted and hollered at length until Tom in his tailored black suit, took his place beside her, taking her hand in his while Trace sat behind his honey oak desk.

"So you two have had a really tough last few months, haven't you? We're specifically talking about December's stalker's trial."

"Yes, it was hard but I had Tom at my side so we got through it together. He's my rock." She answered as Tom brought their joined hands to his lips, smiling.

"Aww look at all that love. Okay, so the trial is now over right? Can you tell us what was the outcome?

"I can now say without a fear of reprisals that Darren Singh has been sentenced to twenty five years in prison with no parole for three counts of attempted murder."

The audience cheered as if this was the first time they'd heard this news. It wasn't. It was played on repeat on every news outlet, magazine and blog.

"Okay that's enough of that. Let's talk about all of the good news happening to you two. Tom, your movie 'The Nation's Princess' has been nominated for numerous awards and is currently number one at the box office." Trace proclaimed causing his audience to once again go wild.

"Yes it is, I'm so honoured to be nominated and pleased that everyone is going out see it."

"Tell us about the movie again?"

"Well it's based on a true story about a bookseller named Daniel Archer, who fell in love with Princess Josephine Von Hassperg of Austria, which sparked an Austrian social revolution when her father refused to allow their request to marry."

"It sounds very romantic."

"It is. I was lucky enough to meet them and they're a very lovely couple."

"Well, I can't wait to see it and I hope you win as many awards as possible." Trace said, sincerely.

"Thanks, Trace. I truly appreciate you saying that." Tom felt oddly touched at his words.

"He's such a gentleman. I like him. Now, Miss December Brown, I heard your latest album went platinum?" Trace inquired, eagerly

"You heard right. I have such amazing fans. It's a truly humbling experience to lay your heart out in a song and for people to understand it."

"And what did you do with the proceeds?" Trace probed, December glared at him briefly. He was fully aware she liked to keep her philanthropic efforts low key but that never stopped Trace.

"I've donated it to the Stroke Awareness foundation and the National Center for Victims of Crime organization."

"That's amazing. Honestly, you could have bought a multimillion dollar vacation home and you chose to donate it all to charity?”

“What's the point of buying frivolous things like vacation homes, when you're in a position to help as many people as you can when you have more than enough to share?” December answered, honestly.

“Wow! That is inspiring. Okay so Tom, hi. You had some news you wanted to share with us? The floor is yours." Trace gestured for Tom to begin.

“Yes actually.” Tom rose from his seat, stood in front of December, relishing her puzzled expression. In one fluid motion he got down on one knee while pulling out a black velvet box. Her hands flew to her mouth in surprise. She looked at Tom with wide shining eyes.

The crowded studio filled with shrieks and delighted applause.

"December Brown, I know the last time we sat beside each other on this couch we were two strangers who were tricked into meeting by well-intentioned friends who thought we'd be perfect for one another. They were right! You're the love of my life. I can't even remember what life was like without you in it and I really don't want to. I should have done this months ago but the moment never seemed right. I wanted it to be memorable and perfect for you. Coming back to where it all began on Trace's show to propose was the only thing that made sense to me. You are the kindest, funniest, sexiest woman I have ever known and I love you from the top of your head to your adorably tiny toes, will you please make me the happiest man in the universe by agreeing to marry me?" Tom implored staring lovingly into December's eyes.

"Yes." She squeaked, nodding wildly.

"Can you repeat that? I don't think they heard you in the back." Trace chirped in.

"Shush. I love you so, so much, of course I'll marry you." She clarified, positively glowing with elation. Flinging herself into Tom's arms she kissed him repeatedly as he tried to slip the ring on her finger without dropping it. The onlookers screamed with joy at her acceptance of the engagement proposal.

"It's absolutely beautiful." She gasped admiring the classically designed princess cut ring with its diamond and platinum band.

"It's a family heirloom." Tom replied happily, thinking of Maurice and Estelle.

No matter how hard he tried Estelle insisted that giving this particular ring to December would make her happier than she thought possible in nearly a decade. It was the first time she'd ever embraced him, speaking to him at length about their late son and how much it would mean to her. Tom now made an effort to send Estelle flowers at least once a week while she, Nunny, his mother and December met up for lunch every month.

"Let me be the first to congratulate you two. I can't wait to go to the wedding will it be a small or lavish?"

"Small" They said simultaneously, already envisioning Sophie, Damien's daughter as flower girl, Clarissa as maid of honor with Nunny walking December down the aisle.

"Tom, you've had more than enough time to decide, so tell us who will you ask to be your best man?" Trace asked, mischievously, knowing fully well that he was putting Tom on the spot. He was just making trouble because he enjoyed it knowing that he wasn't in the running for the position.

Trace was right, Tom had figured out who he wanted as his best man and although he and Peter were making great strides in their friendship he wasn't the person Tom had in mind. Along with Damien, Peter and Trace would be his groomsmen, if they agreed.

"Terrence Mitchell." Tom announced, a loud shout of shock was heard from backstage.

"Terrence?" Trace repeated, he would have bet money that Tom would have picked Maurice.

"Yes, he's December's stylist but we've ended up spending so much time together that we've become great friends. He's honest and hilarious and the only man I've ever loved outside of my manager, Maurice. So, Terrence, what do you think? Will you be my best man?" Tom offered with a winsome grin.

The Camera panned to a sobbing Terrence who nodded vigorously. Tom stood up, unhooked his microphone and strode over to hug him.

"Oh my God, this is the best thing I've ever seen in my life. Clarissa, I hope you're watching!" December beamed with pleasure.

The camera panned back to Trace as the show's producer pointed at his watch who still looked delighted and flabbergasted.

"Um Wow! Thanks for joining us on the best ever episode of Trace Randall Tonight. See you next time."

Book Club Discussion Guide

The Trouble with Romance
by Tamara Philip

(1)　Have you ever played matchmaker? How did it work out?

(2)　The matchmaking seems to have worked out for December and Tom, but what made them decide to play matchmaker with Clarissa?

(3)　What character(s) did you identify with most?

(4)　Where did... how did Clarissa become so cynical about love?

(5)　If you had to describe this book in just one word, what would it be?

(6)　Is Peter the right man for Clarissa?

(7)　When did you realize Clarissa and Peter had a chance of their own HEA?

(8)　Do you believe in fate when it comes to romance?

BONUS

Have Love

originally published in the Holiday Special,
This Season...
with Neva Squires-Rodriguez

by

Tamara Philip

Have Love
by Tamara Philip

Bookstore owner, Danny Archer has always led a quiet unassuming life but when the mysterious Josephine, enters his shop, it's love at first sight.

With Christmas right around the corner and a little help from his twin sister, it seems like a dream come true.

But will the secret that she's harboring leave them heartbroken for the Holidays or will love find a way?

Chapter One

"Oh God, now I'm a stalker." Danny lamented, shaking his head in dismay.

"Why did I even let you talk me into coming here?"

Daniella laughed at his misery.

"You're not a stalker, you big baby! This is a mall! Lots of people come here, you know? I heard it was a booming enterprise." She said sarcastically, leaning forward to flutter her fingers against a silk scarf hanging on the closest kiosk to her. Her twin brother, Daniel was both her best friend in the whole world and the biggest worry wart in worry wart history. She usually convinced him around to her way of thinking by ignoring his whining.

"Ooh! Do you think Mom would want one of these for Christmas? What about Grandma? She could be trendiest granny at the nursing home."

"Don't change the subject! You convinced me to come in here for one sole purpose and that was to stalk the object of my affection. See? I'm calling her an object now. I'm such a creep!" He stood in front of his sister with wide, imploring eyes, looking genuinely upset. Daniella rolled her eyes at his antics.

"Danny, get it together. She's not going to think you're a creep. Hell, she probably doesn't even know you exist."

"Oh thanks, Sis! That makes me feel so much better. Ugh, why do I even listen to you?"

"Because I'm your sister and I'm brilliant? Oh my god, is that a pizza cone?" Daniella shrieked, pulling him along with her at breakneck speed into the "As Seen on TV" store. Seeing her the way she was right now, no one would guess that Daniella Helfenbein nee Archer, was a successful police detective. Most people just assumed that she was a lawyer because she loved to argue so much; however, right now, in her childish glee over an ice cream cone shaped object that could be filled with pizza toppings, she just looked like his pain in the butt twin sister.

"Daniella, be serious!" Danny started but she impatiently cut him off.

"No, you be serious. You own the bookstore that the girl of your dreams frequents every Wednesday and Saturday. The very same bookstore that she's probably in right now, sitting there on the couch like she always does, reading some terrible, terrible book. By the way, she really has bad taste." Daniella made a face that had her brother doing a smirk-eye roll combination that he seemed to use solely when she was around.

"Anyway, you finally have a day off, Danny. The first one in the four years since you've opened, so take advantage of it, go find her. Just so we're clear, I'm not letting you leave this mall until you talk to her. I'm more than prepared to leave my child at her ballet class longer than necessary. And I'll make sure to blame you for my lateness."

"Ugh, I know you're right but I can't. Maybe liking her from afar is good enough?" Danny clawed through his shaggy ginger colored mane, nervously. He hadn't expected to be around people that day, so he looked like a mess, with a washed out uncombed hair and a wrinkled pair of jeans on.

He'd planned to veg out in front of the television and catch up on his shows on Netflix when Daniella had come barging into his apartment demanding that he go last minute Christmas shopping with her. When he'd casually mentioned to her that it was only December tenth, the look she gave him, well… he feared for his life. So when she threw his coat at him, he went with her quietly. If he'd known what she had in mind, Danny would have tried to look his best.

"Shush! look, she's coming out of the bookstore now. What's she doing?" Daniella asked squinting in confusion. The siblings stood side by side in the middle of the busiest part of the mall corridor, watching with rapt interest as Danny's dream girl stopped in the middle of the mall and searched around for something inside her satchel-style bag that was slung diagonally across her chest.

"There's something almost regal about her, isn't there? I mean look at her posture. Her poise, it's beautiful. She's beautiful." he said wistfully. The girl in question straightened up, tossing her cascading curls across one shoulder in one smooth move. Her dark hair complimented her dark-gold complexion and pink glossy lips.

Even Daniella had to admit she was stunning in a classic way.

"Uh okay, sure. Whatever! Seriously she's just standing there looking around. Do you think she's lost or that she's waiting for someone? This could be your moment to help her find what she's looking for. Go!"

Danny took a step forward but stopped as a guy not much older than them, carrying what looked like two medium sized easels under his arms, approached the curvy brunette. They smiled at each other in way that caused Danny's heart to lodge in his throat and constrict.

"Is that her boyfriend?" he croaked out. He knew Daniella wouldn't know any more than he did, but he had to ask anyway.

She squeezed his hand in sympathy, choosing to remain silent for once in her sassy life. Instead, she continued staring along with Danny as the man with the easel which now didn't look like an easel after all, handed one to Dream Girl who smiled and thanked him. She then slid it over her head, as did her acquaintance, before they parted ways with a wave.

"God, isn't her smile the best thing ever?" Danny mused aloud.

Daniella craned her neck to read the sign on the small sandwich board that they both now donned. A second later she cackled loudly.

"What! What is it?'

"It's your lucky day, that's what, brother of mine. Your future girlfriend is wearing a 'HUG Me' sign. Isn't that awesome?" she clapped her hands excitedly, beaming widely at him.

"A hug me sign? What's a- oh my God! No way!" Danny said, in disbelief.

"I know right? Now let's go get you a hug."

Chapter Two

"I can't go now. It'll be weird being the first person. Let's just wait a few minutes."

Daniella rolled her eyes and nodded in reluctant agreement. The twins chuckled when three boisterous toddlers attacked her legs with aggressive cuddles, causing her to burst out in surprised laughter. The tinkling sound of her delight had Danny smiling goofily as he watched the scene unfold. They 'aww'ed when she shared a group hug with an elderly couple but when a line of teenaged boys headed her way, Daniella decided it enough was enough and forcibly dragged him nearer.

"Today's the day, Daniel Leon Archer! Go meet my future sister-in-law." Daniella pushed him roughly which ended up with him nearly knocking into someone.

Danny spun around already apologizing for his clumsiness, which would be easier to do than trying to explain to a stranger that his sister was a brute.

"It's alright. You didn't even touch me. Oh, it's you! The one from the book store!" Her sparkling caramel-colored eyes lit up as she looked at him. Danny smiled widely at her in relief, over the moon at the fact that she knew he existed after all.

"Is that your sister?" She asked, looking pointedly over his shoulder. Danny turned around to find Daniella not even 10 feet away, staring intently at them her hands clasped and a crazed glint her eyes.

"I wish I had a sister." she said wistfully, he noticed an accent but couldn't place it.

"How'd you know she was my sister?"

"You look both familiar. I mean alike…similar!" she sputtered, her flawless brown skin darkening with rosy tones. She caught Daniella's exaggerated scowl at her words.

"Oh no… I don't mean to say you look like a man. It's just that you look like the masculine and feminine version of one another. Same features but placed in the right way. The same eyes and hair color… I'm making such a fool of myself." She covered her face with her hands in embarrassment.

Danny smiled kindly at her, hardly hearing a word she said. He was just happy that she was talking in his direct vicinity. From childhood, anyone who had ever met Danny and his sister always remarked on how much they looked like one another. From their rich red hair to their dark green eyes, even their lean, lanky build; they mirrored one another. However, that's where the similarities stopped. Where Daniella was outspoken and honest to a fault, Danny was cautious and sweet-natured. He put strangers at ease while Daniella put them on guard, which served them well in their chosen professions.

"You're both so dorky and adorable, I love it. Listen, I get it, you mean you think we're both hot right?" Daniella supplied, with a twinkle of mischief in her eye.

"Yes! Wait-- no! I mean, yes! You're both very attractive, yes." Her embarrassment seemed to grow as the conversation continued.

"We get that all the time, don't we, Danny? So you're smart and have good taste… what's your name?" Daniella gave Danny a not so subtle wink that had him face palming.

"Josephine."

"That's a lovely name. Can I call you Josie? "

"Daniella, I think we should go now."

"No, I don't mind. I'm not accustomed to nicknames but I like it!" She looked genuinely delighted at the prospect.

"Really? That's weird, but anyway, I'm Daniella and this is my twin brother, Daniel. Everyone calls him Danny though. He owns the bookstore that you go to all the time."

"Oh, so you've noticed…" Josephine blushed, avoiding Danny's appreciative gaze.

"Well, my brother definitely has." Daniella earned an elbow nudge to her side.

"Ow! I mean, we sure have. It's a small bookstore in a small town, so you know how that goes."

"Well it is my favorite place here in Beltsville. I can't believe you own it."

Danny smiled gratefully at her, finally catching her eye. She smiled back shyly at him.

"Yeah we've been open for nearly 3 years. It was a dream of mine."

"Why do you always buy those awful books? I mean out of all of them, why do you pick the ones with the worst blurb on the back cover? I've literally cringed reading those few lines. Let's not even talk about some of those titles." Daniella butted in, ignoring Danny's pleading look for her to get lost.

Josie laughed in recognition. "Oh, I purchase them for my body- um my uncle, Oliver. He always says that he'll read anything and everything so I've been trying to test his limits. And his patience as he so kindly informed after my last purchase."

Danny grinned "I don't blame him. That one was called the 'Sycophant's Altruistic Decision', I believe."

Josephine laughed, "I cannot believe you remembered that. The evidence against me sounds pretty damning when you put it that way, doesn't it?"

"Where are you from?" Daniella interjected yet again as they shared another chuckle. "I noticed the accent. It's not exactly British, is it?"

"No, not exactly. I did my schooling there but I'm Austrian. Have you ever been?"

"Whoa! Really? You don't really look Austrian. No offense."

"Daniella, shush." Danny knew his sister was a busybody but this was getting to be too much. Josephine's smile faded slightly at the edges for an instant.

"Ah yes, well the brown skin is a courtesy of my mother's side of the family."

"Hey buddy, you gonna hug her or what? You're holding up the line" A booming male voice shouted from behind.

"Wait your turn!" Daniella shouted back.

"You've been talking to her for like 5 minutes. It's a hug, not a damn conference." The man responded just as loudly.

"Don't make me come back there." Daniella threatened. Josie and Danny watched it all unfold in shocked amusement.

"So Josie, when do you finish up with this hugging strangers thing?"

"In about forty five minutes. I change places with Aurelia at that point."

"Good, Danny will meet you at the front of the bookstore then. He's going to ask you out for coffee now. It's been a pleasure to meet you, Josie. We'll see each other again soon. Bye! Hurry up, Danny!"

Josie stared after her, entirely baffled. She turned to Danny with a quizzical look.

"Did I miss something?"

"No, you didn't. She's bossy like that all the time. I'm so sorry."

Josie's eyes brightened with understanding. "So… about this coffee invitation?"

Danny sputtered with relief. "Oh my god! You're actually willing to go out with me? Even after my crazy sister? I swear she won't be there."

"Well, since you promise… I'm just kidding, she's lovely. She reminds me of my father actually. And yes, I'll meet you in less than hour. After I deal with the hordes, obviously." She motioned towards the growing line behind him. Danny turned to look.

"Yikes. I'm so sorry again. Do you need me to stay and help? I can hug some of them for you?"

"That's very kind of you to offer. But I'll be fine. Besides, your sister is waiting for you."

"Are you sure? Okay. Well, good luck. I'll see you later then?" He asked hopefully.

"Yes, it's a date." She smiled wanly at him one last time before stepping around him to the impatient group awaiting her.

"I apologize for the delay everyone! Who wants to cuddle first?" She announced, loudly to the small crowd.

Chapter Three

"She said yes! We're going for coffee!" Danny said as he jogged up to catch up with his sister's long strides. Even in heels, Daniella walked faster than anyone he'd ever met.

"Well duh, did you think she was going to say no?"

"For a second there? Yes! You really need to take the interrogating strangers thing down a notch, Dan! You could have scared her off." Danny admonished.

"Please. If it wasn't for me, you'd still be pining for her like some junior high school boy with his neighbor's hot mom." Daniella replied, dismissively.

"No way! I was going to talk to her soon. You don't know my plans." He pouted, knowing she was right about him.

"Yes way. I know you! You were going to pine and then whine for years about the girl that got away."

"Nope. I was going to ask her out on Tuesday!"

"Tuesday? Yeah right. Probably a random Tuesday- thirty years from now!" Daniella scoffed.

"Just say 'Thank you' and buy me an extra nice Christmas present and we'll call it squaresies."

"Fine! Thank you for being overbearing and pushy. Thank you for not knowing when to take a hint. Thank you for- ow." Danny held his abdomen where Daniella elbowed him.

"You deserved that. And you're very welcome. Now I need to go Wiki Austria because all I know about that place is Arnold Schwarzenegger and that it's not Germany."

"Why? I'll just ask Josephine when I see her in about, um…25 minutes."

"There's something not exactly odd about her, but something is definitely different. I mean that bag she has is a genuine Birkin and not a knock off. The one she had in particular, I used Google, by the way to verify this, costs nearly a hundred and fifty thousand dollars, Danny. Those adorable ankle boots she was wearing? You don't even want to know. And I sincerely doubt that all the people from wherever she's from in Austria have a bodyguard when they travel."

"What are you talking about? What body guard? She was alone."

"Did you even listen? Her Uncle Oliver? hello? She corrected herself from saying bodyguard but I heard."

"Daniella, it doesn't matter. Stay out of this. Please! Stay out of this. I'd rather ask her myself instead of snooping around."

"I'm not snooping. It's research. Stop looking at me like that." Green eyes identical to her own glared at her until she threw her hands up in surrender.

"Okay, okay. I'll let you find out more about her. But you have to tell me everything, okay? And don't forget Gwen's ballet recital is Sunday afternoon."

"I won't. Promise! I'll be there." Danny opened her car door and gave her a quick peck on the cheek.

"Good. We're going out for dinner afterwards. Call me tonight and tell me everything."

"Yeah, yeah! Just drive safe, nosey."

She beeped her horn as she drove out of the parking lot.

"Crap. She was my ride." Danny grumbled to no one in particular. He sighed and quickly calculated how long it would take to go home, get his car and be back in time for his coffee date. "Damn, 5 minutes to spare is cutting it close but worth it in case Josephine needs a ride home. Why am I talking to myself in a parking lot?"

He hailed a cab and willed himself to stay calm during the seemingly endless taxi ride to his apartment.

"You're late." Josephine commented tapping her wrist with a wry smile.

"I know! I'm sorry. I had to go get my car because Daniella drove us here an-" Danny explained, still out of breath from running through the mall. She looked him up and down, quizzically.

"Have you changed your outfit?"

"Uh."

She smiled knowingly when he hesitated.

"And put on cologne?"

"Can I pretend that I just smell like this naturally to get cool points?"

Josephine laughed, which was music to his burning red ears.

"So, um, do you need a foot rub?" Danny blurted out randomly, as they stared awkwardly at each other, neither knowing what to do or say next.

"I'm sorry, what?" She tilted her head, puzzled but expectant. A tiny unsure smile played upon her lips as she waited for his reply.

"Because you've been running through my mind for a while so, um, your feet must be tired?"

"Oh! Oh, Dear!" Josephine covered her mouth with her hand in mock horror.

"I'm sorry, Daniel but that was really, very terrible."

"Um I can't believe I just said that." Danny mumbled, shamefaced yet sporting a goofy grin.

"Yes, it was quite horrible." She replied, grinning widely back.

"That was just my attempt at breaking the ice, okay? I'm so much better than that." He laughed, pleased with himself that he successfully put her at ease, while Josephine tried and failed to control helpless giggles.

"It worked. The ice has completely melted away." She sighed, contentedly. They started walking in amiable silence, not sure where to go but a stroll at that moment seemed appropriate.

"Listen, I'm sorry about earlier. My sister comes on a little strong but she's really sweet if you give her a chance." She waved his apology off with a shake of her head.

"I like her. I doubt anyone tells her what to do. She knows her own mind, as well as yours." Josephine teased, tucking her hands into her dark red coat.

"You aren't kidding there. So are you hungry? Would you like to get some lunch or an early dinner or just coffee?

"Can we share a banana split?" she asked hopefully.

"Um sure, it's the middle of winter but okay." Danny agreed, uncertainly.

"I saw it in a film on television last night. I know it sounds odd for you but I've never had one before." She confessed, sheepishly tugging on a lock of her hair. Danny smiled sympathetically.

"Well then if the lady wants a banana split then that's what we're going to have."

"How very gallant of you, sir." Josephine chirped, accepting the elbow he offered, looping her arm through his. He winked at her and flexed his bicep reveling in the brief flustered look on her face before she looked away, as he lead them through the mall.

"What's it like in Austria at Christmas time?"

"Oh it's wonderful, Daniel! The Christmas markets! The food! The carols on Christmas Eve! It's my favorite time of year. This is the first time I've been far from home at this season." Josephine admitted her voice filled with wistful melancholy.

"I bet you're homesick, but at least you get to enjoy the holidays in a different way." Danny offered in consolation. She nodded in agreement even if she didn't look very convinced.

"What's your favorite part of Christmas?"

"The forgiveness…" Josephine answered absent-mindedly.

"Forgiveness? I thought you'd say gifts or something." Danny shot her a bemused look.

"Oh yes, yes. That's what I meant to say." She amended hurriedly.

"Uh Okay… well, I love the music. I could listen to Christmas songs all year long." He hummed along to "Jingle Bells" badly, in an attempt to cheer Josephine up. She shook her head in dismay, trying hard not laugh again.

"Even though they've played them constantly since November?"

"Yes! Especially because of that. And we can't forget about my fixation with festive sweaters."

"I love festive sweaters too!" Josephine gasped, obviously elated, and began to dramatically unbutton her coat. She held the fabric apart to reveal a multicolored scenic winter wonderland reindeer embroidered sweater that on its best day would be considered tacky, but the absolute beaming pride on Josephine's face was his favorite.

"You wear that shirt really, really well, Josephine." Danny said smiling indulgently at her.

"Thank you! My landlord's mother made it for me. She's very good with knitting." she announced happily. "Would you like her to make you one? She sells lots of things from the back of her car. It's very convenient."

"Oh no, no. I don't think I could pull it off as well as you do." Danny bit the inside of his cheek trying not to laugh. Nevertheless his eyes still twinkled with mirth.

"You're laughing at me! I can see it in your eyes. I have four more of these! Don't laugh!" Josephine playfully scolded him as he gave up the ghost and cackled loudly.

"I'm sorry you just looked so cute showing it off." He explained, wiping his eyes, still chuckling.

"You tricked me." she pouted and, just as dramatically as before, re-buttoned her coat.

"I couldn't help it! Honestly though I own one with a light-up Santa Claus on it, so I can't judge."

Josephine giggled at the image of the towering 6'3 Danny in such a sweater.

After polishing off a banana split between them, they sat chatting in a small booth side by side. Danny rested his elbow on the table, his body turned to face her.

"So tell me about yourself. How did you become one of those hugging people?"

"I hadn't realized that was an actual thing to do until I saw Dwayne and Aurelia offering the service the weekend before last. After I hugged them, I asked if I could join and well, here we are."

"That's really sweet. Are you a natural hugger or something?"

"I believe I am. I didn't have the most affectionate of childhoods but I loved hugging all of those strangers today. So yes, I shall say I am. Are you?"

"Am I a natural hugger? Definitely! I give the best hugs or so everyone tells me."

"You look very inviting. Never mind, I didn't say that." Josephine covered her mouth, shaking her head in disbelief at her own words. Danny hid his grin and quickly changed the subject.

"You have such a great smile, Daniel. You should smile more."

Danny blushed a deep red and leaned across the booth towards her.

"Josephine, listen I-"

"Daniel, I'm so sorry but I have to get going now. It's getting late and I have to meet my uncle in a few minutes."

"Really? Okay let me just pay for this stuff and I'll walk you out." He started to slide out of his seat but she stopped him.

"There's no need but thank you, Daniel. My Uncle is just down the hall."

"Oh. Okay. Can I call you tonight?" He felt deflated that their date was ending so abruptly.

"I'd love that." Josephine quickly wrote down her phone number and kissed him on the cheek.

"I'm so sorry. I had so much fun talking to you. Bye."

Danny grabbed her hand, impulsively, and she turned back to face him.

"Wait. Have dinner with me tomorrow. Please."

"Yes" she answered breathlessly, smiling widely. "I'll meet you in front of your bookstore tomorrow at five. Is that okay?"

"That sounds perfect." Danny stood up, still holding her hand. He leaned down and kissed the palm of her hand.

"Bye, Josephine." She looked up into his eyes, in a dreamlike daze. She shook herself out of her stupor, grabbed her coat and bag, and stumbled through the crowd of late afternoon shoppers as Danny stood staring longingly after her retreating form.

Chapter Four

The next evening, Danny showed up with a dozen red roses when she arrived at their agreed meeting place.

"These are gorgeous. Thank you, Daniel." Josephine sniffed the flowers deeply, her eyes fluttering close. When she opened them she found herself staring into Danny's as he gazed down at her adoringly.

"They aren't half as gorgeous as you." He said, taking her hand in his as they walked out of the mall into the parking lot towards his car. Josephine halted mid-step, deciding suddenly to take a leap of faith.

She'd stayed up most of the night before watching "Love Actually" and maybe it was a little foolish to follow directions from a movie, but she didn't know when she'd have a chance like this again. She was in a foreign country far from home, with a man who made her heart flutter holding her hand. She willed her heart to stop pounding so loudly.

"Josephine, are you okay?" Danny asked, worriedly.

"Daniel, I have to tell you something. And it may be a little forward of me to say it, but I study you while I'm at the bookstore pretending to read. I am quite fond of your face and your smiles are the best part of my day." She exhaled and closed her eyes for a moment before turning to look at him for a response. Her spine was rigid with nerve but she still felt a deep sense of relief at her admission.

"You noticed me?" Danny looked at her, confusion and disbelief etched on his face.

"Yes." She said slowly, feeling slightly less sure of herself than she did only seconds before.

"Let me be clear, I could have asked you out over a month ago and you would have said yes?"

"Yes, if you had asked…"

"But you're so beautiful…" Danny looked genuinely surprised at her admittance. Josephine touched his hand to get his attention and the feel of her warm skin against his finally brought him to his senses.

"Josephine, from the second I saw you, I couldn't get you out of my mind. You're the girl of my dreams. And I didn't want to tell you that in the middle of a parking lot, but you're the best part of my day too." He said honestly, placing his hand over hers. They smiled brightly at each other, each feeling a weight lift off their shoulders as they admitted what was in their hearts.

They sat across from each other in a little booth in a tiny steakhouse restaurant within the mall. Hands still intertwined, Danny placed a soft kiss on the back of Josephine's.

"Do you attend Christmas mass?" She asked out of the blue.

They'd talked for hours about anything and everything that came to mind, not wanting their impromptu date to end. From her childhood in various boarding schools in Europe, to how his parents and grandmother, who lived in Boca Raton, Florida, rarely visited because they hated the cold weather. Danny hardly noticed that they skirted around parts of her personal story and focused mainly on his.

He didn't pry and she didn't offer, and truly he didn't care one way or the other, just as long as she was near him.

"No, I'm not very religious."

"You don't have to be very religious to go to Mass, especially at Christmas and Easter. I love it because that's when people are at their best. Wearing their finery and with such hope and love for their fellow man. I always cry then, but only happy tears. Is that odd?"

"I've got to tell you, before today, I never even thought about it. But now I'd love to go with you. I'm pretty sure if you wanted to go donkey racing, I would say yes and mean it."

Josephine giggled, tossing her lush ringlets of hair behind her. Danny reached over and twirled a strand around his fingers. He noticed the twinkling gemstones in her earrings and sighed.

"Not that I'm complaining or anything, but out of all places how did you end up here in Bridgeville? Why not somewhere glamorous? Like Los Angeles or New York City?"

She regarded him carefully, the easy smile she'd had moments before slid into a cautious replacement. From her reaction Danny gathered that he'd asked a touchy question but it was something that weighed on his mind the night before while he laid in bed thinking about their ice cream date.

"My father recommended Bridgeville." Josephine answered impassively.

"Really? Why of all places would he send his gorgeous daughter to Delaware?"

"His reasons are his own, which he hasn't informed me of. Although, I'm sure some sort of business venture played a part in his choosing such a...random location." Her tone was cool, bordering on icy, leaving no mistake that she wanted him to change the subject.

159

Have Love

Danny was well aware that he was pushing his luck, he could see it clear as day but he couldn't have survived with a sister like Daniella, if he hadn't picked up a trick or two on how to be pushy and slightly ruthless when he wanted an answer.

"A business man? He must be doing pretty well right? I mean look at you. You have the air of 'Heiress' about you."

"I'm sorry but why are you asking me these questions?" She pulled away from him, politely but nonetheless taken aback. Josephine's hurt expression jolted Danny back to his senses.

"I screwed that up, didn't I? Listen, I'm sorry! I was rude and nosey. I just wanted to get to know more about you. Where you come from, you know?" He wanted to reach out for her but decided against it when he saw that his apology wasn't enough.

"I didn't mean to upset you or sound like I was accusing you of anything, but my dad was a jeweler for years and, well, long story short…you've got real diamonds and sapphire earrings on. Your coat tag says Oscar De La Renta, and not to mention your bag from the other day was worth a butt load of money. So I'm guessing you're the daughter of an oil tycoon or something?"

"Austria doesn't have oil tycoons. However, they do have Hedge funds and I am a Hedge fund analyst by trade, albeit for the family business. I do quite well for myself via that, so I can afford to wear what I wear." Josephine informed him, sitting up ramrod straight, tension emanating off her body in waves, still she didn't look upset, just guarded and more than a little resentful.

"You don't have to tell me anymore until you feel like it okay? I'm sorry. We were having such a great time and I ruined it."

"No, don't be sorry. It's my own fault. Yes, technically I am from a wealthy family but it's not what you think. It's a long story and I doubt you'll believe me right off the bat…" She explained, looking uncomfortable.

"You can tell me anything. I just want to know more about you." Danny said earnestly, sincerely, imploringly, his eyes never leaving hers. Josephine hesitated. She wanted to tell him but she didn't want to spoil the illusion that her secret allowed her to have. Fortunately, her cell phone buzzed a text message at that moment. She pulled it out of her bag and glanced at the message. Color faded from her face.

"What? What is it? What's wrong?" The concern in Danny's voice brought Josephine back to attention. She slapped a forced serene look on her face.

"It's nothing. I just…I just have to go right now." She stated in a calm, controlled tone, grabbing her handbag and coat.

"Are you sure? Do you need a ride somewhere? I can take you home." Danny offered.

"No, thank you. My ride will be here shortly. Thank you for a lovely time, Daniel." She smiled sweetly at him, but he could see something was still bothering her.

"I'll call you tonight? So I can check on you?" He didn't want to push any further, sensing that he'd nearly ruined things already. His heart sank when Josephine hesitated for an instant before nodding.

"Goodbye, Daniel." She leaned down and kissed him softly on the cheek before walking quickly out of the restaurant's double doors.

Chapter Five

Dinner at Gwen's favorite restaurant was normally something Danny looked forward to, but after screwing things up with Josephine, he would have rather been at home sulking.

"So, she hasn't returned any of your calls?" Daniella's husband, Ricky, asked as he stuffed himself with garlic bread.

"Nope! I should have known when she pretty much bolted out of there." Danny grumbled, feeling sorry for himself as he speared his spinach ravioli.

"Why are you already losing hope? The way she looked at you, the way you looked at each other? I refuse to believe that it's already over between you just because you asked a few questions." Daniella glared at her brother, willing him to have a little more faith than that.

"You weren't there. She looked so upset after I mentioned it and then she got that text message and it was game over, man!"

"Uncle Danny, Christmas time is when miracles happen. You just have to believe." Gwen said as she dipped her French fries into her grisly ketchup and maple syrup concoction. Danny smiled lovingly at his niece.

"You know something, Gwenny-bear, you're pretty smart for a four year old." He said tickling her sides.

"I'm not four, I'm eight" She giggled loudly, instantly brightening Danny's mood. He sat back up in his seat and glanced out of the large window that they sat beside.

"Look, it's Josephine!" He exclaimed excitedly, motioning out to the sidewalk where Josephine was engaged in a heated discussion with an older, burly gentleman with dark mahogany skin. They both seemed out of place for Bridgeville in all its small town glory. Their clothing was both expertly tailored, him in a Herringbone charcoal gray three piece suit while Josephine's plum colored dress coat obscured most of her attire, her matching stilettos gleaming in the sunlight.

"I wonder how she got her hair into that chignon. It looks absolutely flawless. Not a single hair is out of place, even this wind." Daniella said in awe.

"I can't believe she's just standing not even 50 feet away, right after you guys lectured me about not giving up." Danny muttered, still watching the two interact.

"See we were right, but maybe you should call her later. She seems a little busy." Daniella warned, craning her neck to get a better view.

"She might need help. He could be some creep following her or something. She's really laying into him by the looks of it." Danny pushed his seat backwards and stood up.

"I'll be right back. Stay here."

He marched out into the blustery December afternoon and hurried over to where the two figures still stood. Although the man towered over Josephine by over a foot, she didn't seem at all wary. The closer Danny got to them, the more snippets of conversation he caught.

"He has sold me, Oliver. Like livestock to the highest bidder."

"Josephine, he simply thinks this is the best thing for you right now."

"The best thing for me? How kind. Who is it to be then? Is he a pig farmer in Bulgaria or is it worse?" She chuckled, humorlessly.

"Josephine, please calm down."

"I am calm, Oliver. I am saddened, though, that he didn't even tell this news to me. He told it to you to pass the message along. It's my life that he's plotting out and he can't even spare me a phone call?"

"You have to understand, your father is under a lot of pressure and perhaps his decision leaves a lot to be desired."

"Precisely, what I think! So I'll need you to arrange a phone call with him. As soon as possible, Oliver!"

"Josephine! Hey! Are you okay?" Danny called out as he stepped in front of her. Her face was twisted in a tortured look of fury and hurt, but at the sight of him and at the sound of his voice, a relieved smile instantly replaced the deep frown. Her anger seemed to quickly recede as she closed the space between them.

"Daniel! What are you doing here?" Josephine surprised him by wrapping her arms around his waist in a tight hug, which he returned without hesitation.

"Are you alright? Need me to get rid of him?" He whispered into her hair, as they embraced.

"I'm sorry, I don't know what came over me." Josephine stepped away from him, suddenly realizing her forwardness in front of Oliver. Danny studied her face for any signs of distress.

"Don't apologize, I liked it." He winked at her and she blushed furiously, her ears reddened at the tips. Oliver cleared his throat loudly.

"Where are my manners? This is Oliver. Oliver, this is the Daniel that I spoke to you about the other day."

Oliver silently glared at Danny's close proximity as he sized him up.

"Don't mind him. He's always rude. It's very nice to run into you, but where is your coat? It's freezing."

"Oh, I saw you out here and I thought I'd say hi. We're having an early dinner to celebrate my niece's ballet recital. We have a table right over there." Danny pointed to the little family restaurant that stood at the corner of the street. "Come join us."

"Oh, I would love to but I wouldn't want to impose." Josephine said politely, as Oliver placed a firm hand at her elbow, attempting to steer her away in the opposite direction.

"No! You won't be imposing. I would really love it if you would come join us…both of you." Danny chanced a look at the looming, impassive, face that continued to stare him down with only the occasional blink to suggest that he wasn't some sort of gargoyle.

"Josephine, we don't have time for this. We still have matters to discuss." Oliver spoke up, looking pointedly at her. She shot him a furiously defiant look.

"Well if you insist, Daniel. Only because you're standing here shivering. Oliver is right, though we cannot stay long."

The older man gritted his teeth in dismay as Danny smiled gratefully at her and led the way.

"Look who's joining us! Josephine and, um, Oliver! You remember Daniella, of course. This is her husband, Ricky, and their daughter, Gwen. We're here celebrating her successful Christmas ballet recital." Danny motioned to the little girl who was busy scribbling away in the restaurant supplied coloring books and her Father, an olive toned balding man who sported a handlebar mustache.

"Hey, nice to meet you both! Danny, here can't stop talking about you! I can see why now." Ricky said as he stuck his hand out to shake. Josephine smiled and shook his hand but Oliver stood behind her like a resentful sentinel.

"Look at her in her little tutu, Oliver! Isn't she lovely? I took ballet too, when I was your age. I was terrible at it, wasn't I, Oliver?" Josephine gushed. The man in question barely contained an eye roll.

"Wow, you're really pretty!" Gwen said breathlessly in response. Josephine's face broke in to a bright smile. She curtsied with a dramatic flourish much to Gwen's ballet enthused delight.

"Nice to see you again, Daniella, you have a beautiful family."

"Josephine! Thanks for joining us. Are you two hungry? I can get some more menus? Ricky, don't just sit there! Pull up a seat for Josie and her friend. Wait...isn't Oliver your uncle or something like that? He looks more like a bodyguard if you don't mind me saying...Sorry, Oliver." Daniella offered up a rueful smile. Oliver narrowed his eyes at her but Josephine patted his arm in consolation.

"No, we've already eaten, thank you. And Oliver is both, really."

"Who is this Josie person?" Oliver whispered harshly into Josephine's ears. His deep, booming voice carried nevertheless.

"Josie is her nickname. I gave it to her yesterday." Daniella informed him, eyeing him shrewdly. Oliver looked back and forth at the two women, completely outraged at the thought.

"You will cease to address her as such, Madam."

"Oliver, please. It's alright." Josephine interceded in a tone that suggested she had to deal with this outburst more times than she cared for.

"No it isn't. You are addressing her highness, Princess Josephine Angela Wilhelmina Charlotte Von Hassperg, daughter of King Constantin the Eighth. Please do not attempt to shorten her name again."

The entire table froze in shock at Oliver's words, except for Josephine, who looked mortified. Gwen broke the silence first.

"Whoa, you're a princess? Like a real live princess? Like Princess Tiana?"

"Honey, she's not really a princess. Oliver is just making a joke." Daniella murmured, studying Josephine's reaction.

"Oliver is correct, Gwen." Josephine averted her gaze from Danny, who made repeated attempts to catch her eye. She'd lose her nerve and bolt out of the restaurant if she did.

"But who is Princess Tiana?" Josephine asked keeping her focus on Gwen. She was stalling for time, knowing it was time to come clean. Especially since she'd spied Daniella typing frantically into her phone from the corner of her eye. She could only assume that she was being Googled.

"She's only the greatest Disney princess ever. I'll tell you all about her later. Can I ask you another question?" Josephine nodded. She didn't want to look at the faces of the other adults at the table, so she kept her focus on the sweet little brunette with the messy bun.

"Of course, Gwen! I'm used to being questioned." She said keeping her tone light. Danny grimaced at the words, knowing she meant them for him.

"If you're a princess, then will you be queen one day?"

"That's a good question, Gwen. I can't wait to hear the answer." Daniella responded, not bothering to look up from the screen she was studying intently. Danny looked around in complete shellshock, while Ricky refocused on the steak before him.

"I am fifteenth in line to the throne. Therefore, I will more than likely never become queen."

"That's okay being queen is probably hard. Princesses are cooler, anyway. Do you live in a castle? Where is your castle? Do you have any brothers or sisters?"

"I don't live in a castle. I live in a very nice house, though, in Austria, where I was born. I'm the only child from the union of my father and his seventh and final wife, Queen Angela; however, I have fourteen siblings in total from his previous marriages."

"Fourteen! Then why did you say you wished you had a sister?" Daniella butted in again, this time actually looking up to cast an accusing glare Josephine's way.

"Fourteen sons. I'm his only daughter and youngest child." Josephine explained. Her eyes wandered over to Danny's. She expected to see disbelief or even betrayal in his eyes, but instead, he looked just as enamored by her as he did the day before. He winked when he caught her gaze and she felt lighter.

"Oh wow! That's a lot of brothers. Danny, you have some work cut out for you. Better start taking some boxing classes to defend yourself. I bet they fall all over themselves trying to play your protectors whenever you bring a guy home, right?" Daniella teased, but Josephine's eyes clouded over with an unknown emotion.

"Unfortunately, we are not close. I was born long after many of them had married or were in the late stages of courtship, you see..."

But Daniella refused to see regardless of how many dirty looks her husband and brother tried to give her. She knew it was an uncomfortable conversation but since Danny was too smitten to question things, she'd have to play the bad guy for a little while longer, just until Josephine passed her test.

"That's no excuse. In fact, that should have made them more protective of you." she insisted, looking directly into Josephine's eyes.

"Gwen baby, here's five dollars. Go play at the arcade that's near the bathrooms, where I can see you." Her daughter didn't bat an eye as snatched the money out of her mother's hands and zigzagged her way to the back of the restaurant. Josephine waited until Gwen was out of earshot before answering.

"I wish that were the case, but I only saw them on the occasions where we needed to interact."

"Your mother should have made them."

"She died in childbirth. And I was the remaining byproduct of his highly controversial marriage to a commoner. Albeit, from one of Benin's oldest political and financial dynasties." Josephine explained with the practiced ease of someone who'd had to repeat something often.

"Oh. I'm sorry." Daniella glanced bashfully at Danny and Ricky, who shot her judging looks.

"It's fine. In any case, my brothers are very traditional aristocrats. From the very color of my skin to my mother's death, I embody everything untraditional to them. Or so I was told in the most diplomatic terms, of course."

"I bet your father dotes on you, especially since you're the only girl."

"Yes." Josephine whispered gloomily, with a faraway look in her eyes. Danny, sensing her mood plummeting further, reached out and squeezed her hand in consolation. She smiled gratefully in return.

"Please tell me he didn't blame you for her death."

"Oh, of course not. We were very close. Everyone said he favored me over my brothers."

"Were? What do you mea-?" Daniella tried to inquire before her brother cut her off.

"Okay, that's enough, Daniella. I think you interrogated Josephine enough. I'm sorry I even let it go on so long."

"Fine, I'm sorry Josephine. I adore you, okay? I even Googled you to see if you were telling the truth, which you were, but I just need to make sure my brother can trust you."

"I understand. I appreciate your candor."

"Good, now I'll interrogate Oliver here instead." She announced spinning around to face the man in question.

Chapter Six

"Ugh! Daniella! Seriously?! That's enough." Danny may have been slow to anger but he knew more than anyone else, how irritating his sister's inquisitive nature could be.

"No, she can ask any question she wants of me." Oliver stated proudly, glaring at everyone at the table.

"Great. How are you her uncle and bodyguard?"

"My sister was her mother. I am our father's sole bastard."

"Illegitimate." Josephine quietly corrected. Oliver smiled fondly at her and lightly touched her cheek. Danny recognized the look as one that Ricky often gave Gwen, the look of utter devotion.

"I was left on his doorstep, abandoned by my mother. Angela fought to keep me in their household and even though she was merely twelve when I was born, she took care of me like I was her own. She was my fierce protector, my defender, and my entire world." Oliver stated, passionately. Josephine took his hand in hers, as he continued on.

"So when the time came for her to wed Josephine's father, she asked me to go with her to Austria and I gladly accepted. There was nothing in Benin for me without her and she knew this."

"Okay so that's the uncle part. When did the burly bodyguard part kick in?"

Ricky sighed in exasperation at his wife's line of questioning, but Daniella ignored him.

"I was only fifteen at the time and eager to prove myself. After speaking to my sister about it, I asked King Constantin to put me into the royal guard training program to be able to protect my sister. I was away finishing up the training when I received news that she had died in childbirth. I was bereft for months, but when I laid eyes on Josephine, I knew it was my duty to protect her as I would have my sister. Now my niece is my home and I would gladly give my life for her."

"That's the most I've ever heard you speak about Mother, Oliver. Thank you." Josephine dabbed at her teary eyes with a napkin.

"I should have told you sooner, Josephine."

"Wow, okay now that was emotional. I'm glad I asked…I feel like we bonded!" Daniella exclaimed. "So who wants cake?"

"I'd love a slice of chocolate cake right now." Josephine replied gratefully.

"Daniel, may I have a word with you privately?"

"Yeah, of course! I'll get my coat." Danny jumped out of his chair, eager to get away from the table and his sister's prying eyes.

Once they were outside and out of earshot, Josephine turned to face him. She took a deep breath, already regretting what she'd have to say.

"Daniel, I'm sorry I didn't return your phone calls and I'm sorry that I didn't tell you about who I was before. I just didn't know how to tell you."

"Listen, don't apologize. I'm wracking my mind wondering how you could have brought it up last night without it coming off as a joke or something. So, yeah, I understand. Well, I don't...but I'm getting there."

"How are you so wonderful? I wish I'd met you earlier." Josephine said forlornly.

"What's wrong with meeting me now?" He winked at her, but she quickly looked away.

"We can only be friends so I don't want you thinking there can be more between us."

"It's too late, I want more. I want us to be more."

"I want that, too. With all of my heart, but I can't."

"Why? Because of royal things?" Josephine shot him an amused look.

"Yes, actually."

"Well, screw that."

"I don't think that's an option." she laughed.

"Yes it is. It's easy, I'll show you how." Danny grinned, winsomely at her.

"How?" Josephine furrowed her brows, skeptically.

"Be my date for Daniella's Christmas party on Saturday night."

"How is that helpful to my 'royal things' problem?"

"Say yes and you'll see." He replied, oozing charm and the promise of a good time.

"I shouldn't."

"Yeah, you should. Please? Pretty please?" Josephine looked away, hiding her smile and vainly attempting to ignore his puppy dog eyes.

"You want to say yes, so say yes!"

"This is a very bad idea, but yes. Yes, I would love to be your date."

"Great. It'll be awesome and you'll forget about your problems, at least for a little while."

Josephine desperately wanted to believe him, although she knew that would not be the case.

"Is Oliver invited too?"

"Sure! He's your uncle, isn't he? Anything you care about, I care about."

"You really shouldn't say things like that, Daniel."

"Why not? I mean it. Josephine, look, I need to get some stuff off my chest, too." He said taking her hand.

"Unless you're going to tell me that you're a long lost prince from the Carpathian Mountains, please don't say any more. I couldn't bear it. Not today, Daniel. I beg of you."

"Okay, okay! It's a little soon for me to tell you anyway. I don't want to scare you off. But, just so you know, one day I will tell you." He cradled her face in his hands. Josephine closed her eyes and reveled in his touch.

"I know."

Chapter Seven

"Where is Josephine? She said she'd be here tonight." Danny paced back and forth in Daniella's kitchen as they prepared for the onslaught of holiday party guests.

"It's still early. Calm down. Why didn't you just pick her up? Are you sure she has the right address? You know how you are with directions."

"I know, that's I used Google maps directions after she said she would rather meet here because she had some things to do before the party."

"See? So stop raising my blood pressure with your pacing. Go make sure Gwen's dressed and ready to come downstairs when the doorbell rings." Daniella admonished as she opened the oven.

"Fine, but I'm pacing upstairs now."

"Whatever, I don't care. Just go away, you're ruining my vol-au-vent mojo." she said, waving him off, impatiently.

Danny forced himself not to call to check on Josephine, but he was buzzing with nervous energy. It had only been a week since that first date with her yet he wanted to tell her how he felt, how he'd felt from the first day she'd wandered into his small bookstore two months earlier. It was love at first sight for him.

Have Love

Danny knew then and there that she was the woman he wanted to marry. After that realization however, nerves had taken over and he became a muted mess whenever she approached the checkout counter. Josephine would thank him with a lingering smile and that would be the highlight of his day. No matter how much he pep-talked himself, he just couldn't work up the courage to actually speak to her. He caught her glancing at him from the corner of his eye sometimes when he'd be busily chatting with his employees or other customers, but no words would come when she stood before him.

However, now because his bossy boots sister couldn't watch him fester any longer, Josephine was in his life and like magic, he could breathe again. He knew Daniella would be expecting amazing gifts for every birthday and Christmas for years to come because of his newfound happiness, but he didn't mind one bit just as long as he could see Josephine walk through that overly decorated threshold all glammed up for the Holiday party.

"Uncle Danny, why are you smiling at the wall?" Gwen asked, tugging on his dark red Christmas sweater to get his attention.

"Huh? What? Oh, no, sorry, I was just daydreaming. I think I heard the doorbell ring like fifty bazillion times since I came up here to get you." He teased.

"No way, it only rang five times. I counted!"

"What? Are you serious? And we're still up here! Let's go see who it is, then!" Danny pretended to race her down the steps, but stayed one step behind to let her win.

He heard the front door open when he reached the bottom step. His heart quickened with hope that it might be Josephine but it was only Marvin and Alberta, the slightly obnoxious neighbors from two houses down.

"Daniel?" Josephine's voice came from behind him. He spun around to see a vision in burgundy that took his breath away. Her gauzy knee length off the shoulder cocktail dress fit her like a dream.

"You're here! I was upstairs. If I knew you were here, I would have been down sooner. Why didn't anyone call me?" His wide grin matched hers, as they stood staring goofily at one another.

"I snuck in with a group of people. I wanted to surprise you."

"Well you did. You look gorgeous. Hmm I wonder…"

"What? What is it?" Josephine asked. Danny took several long strides towards her, pulling her into an abrupt hug while nuzzling her ticklish neck. She giggled loudly. He let her go and stepped back, putting his hands into the pockets of his black slacks, nonchalantly.

"Yup, I was right. You smell incredible."

"Danny, stop harassing the guests." Daniella called out, followed by a flash and click.

"Oh my God, you two look so adorable staring at each other in this photo. You should use it in your engagement announcements."

"Let me see!" Danny said reaching for the camera

"No, you'll see it tomorrow with all the other pictures. Now go mingle." she admonished, hiding the camera behind her back.

"Daniel, we brought along a gingerbread house. Come see!" Josephine held out one delicate hand and he took it happily, as she led them into the kitchen where Oliver awaited them.

He was sipping eggnog out of a Santa's face mug, trying to keep a serious expression on his face as Gwen talked his ear off.

"Whoa, did you make this? It looks amazing." Danny said, staring at the elaborate two story Victorian mansion made out of gingerbread cookies and icing.

"I wish. It was Oliver. He worked tirelessly on it all day. Isn't it wonderful?"

"Yes. Very! Hey Oliver, those are some skills you have there." Oliver begrudgingly nodded his head in response.

"Aunt Josie, Aunt Josie you're here!" Gwen squealed, she ran and launched herself at Josephine who opened her arms in time to catch her. She picked up the little girl with a puzzled expression. She looked to Danny for answers while Gwen made herself comfortable by wrapping her long gangly legs around her waist.

"She decided she likes the idea of having a real-life princess in the family. Apparently, you're Aunt Josie now." Danny shrugged, hiding his smile behind a chocolate covered pretzel stick.

"Is that true, Gwen? But we've only just met." Josephine asked she felt small arms wrap around her neck. Gwen buried her face into her hair and nodded, vigorously.

"I think she's feeling a little shy now that you know."

"No! I'm not shy, she just smells nice."

"Oh, well excuse me. How about answering Josephine then?"

"I want you to be my aunt. I don't have any aunts because Daddy doesn't have any sisters. Neither does mommy. Also Uncle Danny loves you, so when you get married, you'll be really family then, right?"

Josephine's eyes grew large and sad as she stared at Danny's hopeful face. She chose her next words carefully.

"I'm honored that you would like to call me Aunt Josie, and I like your uncle very much, too."

"Yay! So I get to be flower girl at your wedding, right? Are you two going to kiss under the mistletoe?" Gwen squirmed out of her arms, pulling them both to the center of the living room where the mistletoe hung above dancing guests.

"Okay, now kiss."

"Um, Gwen, I don't think that's how it works."

"I've seen it on TV. If you stand underneath it, you have to kiss someone. So kiss." She insisted pushing them closer together.

"I am so sorry about this. She's just as bad as her mother."

"I see this."

"We don't have to do this, you know."

"I am aware of that."

"Okay so..."

"So kiss me th-" Josephine's words were cut off midway by the press of Danny's lips against hers. She smiled and deepened the embrace as she wrapped her arms around his neck. It was the sweet, melt your insides kind of kiss that she'd hoped it would be.

Pretending to care about buying books for two months straight so you can see the man of your dreams can become tiresome while you wait for him to gather the nerves to ask you out, but it was all worth it for a kiss like this one.

The kiss ended with a breathless sigh and a round of applause.

"Oh God, why is everyone I know so embarrassing?" Danny groaned, resting his cheek against hers.

"I was starting to wonder that." she mused, glowing with love.

181

Chapter Eight

Danny hummed 'Jingle bells' happily as he drove over to his sister's house on his lunch break, to drop off his brother in law's Christmas present that he'd been hiding for her. Ricky would still be at the high school finishing up his end of term duties as principal, Daniella was on duty at the police department, and Gwen would be with Josephine getting manicures, with Oliver grumpily tagging along. Just thinking about the fact that she was now part of his life had Danny grinning from ear to ear. Adoring her from afar didn't even compare to finally being able to actually be with her. They'd seen each other every day since the Christmas party and each time he'd found himself falling harder for her. And he wasn't the only one. Gwen was practically Josephine's shadow, following her everywhere, attempting to copy the way she did her hair and mimicking her mannerisms. The best part for Danny though was how Josephine seemed to bloom when her mini me was near.

In the weeks that they'd known each other, Josephine had thoroughly spoiled Gwen with lavish gifts and rapt adoration. She'd told him the other night, as they cuddled in bed that his niece was like the baby sister she'd always wanted only better. It wasn't a surprise to him that Josephine had become almost a staple in Daniella's home while he was at work. His sister was more than happy for the free babysitting and even Oliver begrudgingly enjoyed Ricky's company since it mostly involved watching the news and grumbling at the state of the world.

To Danny this was his idea of heaven and better than any gift he could receive on Christmas day.

After parking his car in the driveway, he unlocked the front door and stepped into the foyer with the large already wrapped package in his arms. Danny had carefully hid it in the hall closet, behind the coats like Daniella instructed when he heard female voices coming from the living room. At first, he thought it was his sister but then he heard the cultured European accent and knew it was Josephine. A grin the size of Kansas appeared on his face as he tiptoed closer to the sounds when something she said stopped him in his tracks.

"I've mislead you, Daniel. I've mislead you and now I'm madly in love with you and there's nothing to be done about it." She loved him back! She was in love with him! Danny's heart swelled to bursting with elation.

"What do you mean, my love?" His niece's faux baritone voice made him snort with silent laughter. Gwen's impression of her uncle was nowhere near accurate but after bursting out in a peal of laughter, Josephine resumed her serious speech.

"I don't want to tell you because it will hurt you that we cannot be together." Danny frowned, the joyful light dimming within his eyes.

"Auntie Josie, I don't like this game anymore. I know I said I would help you but now it's getting too sad." He listened to Josephine's footsteps as she crossed the carpeted floor to where Gwen sat. He moved into the doorway and watched as she consoled the little girl, her back facing him as they embraced.

"Oh sweet girl, I'm sorry. You're right, I'm sorry. I shouldn't have involved you with this. Thank you for being so lovely and trying to help this confused soul of mine."

"If you tell me what's wrong, maybe I could help you?" Danny said as he stepped into the room. They turned to stare at him, one tear filled pair of baby blue eyes, who now knew too much of grown-up affairs, and the other a tormented honey brown.

"Uncle Danny! Don't be mad at her, I begged and begged her to tell me what was wrong. She was really sad so I told her to rehearse what she wanted to say and it'll come easier. Just like Mommy showed me that time I had to talk in front of the whole school. Remember, Uncle Danny?" Gwen pleaded, tears spilling down her round, young face.

"Yeah, I remember, sweetie. I'm not mad so you don't need to worry. Why don't you go up to your room and watch some TV or something? I think Josephine needs to talk to me about some things."

She turned a concerned look at Josephine, who simply smiled sweetly at her and nodded.

"I didn't mean to upset her, Daniel. I would never do that on purpose." Josephine said as soon as they heard the sound of Gwen's bedroom door close.

"I know. Tell me what's wrong?" Danny suddenly felt tired. He didn't really want to hear the ending of the conversation that he heard start before, but he knew he had to.

Josephine crossed the space between them and took his large hand in hers. He felt her smooth, cool palms against his as she put their joined hands to her lips. She looked at him with large eyes brimming with sorrow. He reached out and gently caressed her face, offering her an encouraging smile.

"I love you." Josephine said softly.

"I love you, too. You know that. Since the first time I laid eyes on you."

"Yes." Her eyes fluttered shut briefly before opening again with a renewed look of determination.

"But we cannot be together."

Danny pulled her to him as he leaned on the arm of the couch.

"So I heard. Now, tell me why?"

Josephine tried to step away but he wrapped his arm around her waist, drawing her back in. He pressed his forehead to her chest, just above her heart.

"You know you can tell me anything, Josephine. Whatever it is, we'll work through it together."

She sighed deeply, running a tentative hand through his silken hair.

"How much did you overhear?"

"Doesn't matter. Just start from the beginning."

"Alright, I have not been entirely honest with you. I have omitted huge truths from my story."

"Okay then, tell me now. All of it."

Danny heard her heartbeat speed up as she inhaled and exhaled a shaky breath. Her body tensed in his arms but he did not release his hold on her.

"I've been in this country for the past few months, not as a vacation or a year abroad, but as a forced sabbatical on orders from my father, King Constantin. I have disgraced the family name and he sent me here with Oliver as my only companion and bodyguard. For these past few months, I have lived as an outcast because of that I have done."

"Well, that's okay. It doesn't matter if you're an outcast here. You don't have to be alone any longer. My family will be your family. Just marry me."

Josephine finally broke away at his words. She could see the sincerity and it only broke her heart further.

"No. No matter how wonderful that sounds, it still cannot be. Please let me finish."

Danny nodded, studying her face but she turned away from him to look out of the window.

"My father has sent word that he is willing to forgive me and accept me back into the family. All I have to do is marry the man he has arranged for me to wed and I would be able to save face."

Danny's heart stopped in his chest but he willed it to carry on with sheer willpower. He took a deep, steadying breath before trusting himself to speak.

"When did you find this out?"

"The day of Gwen's ballet recital when you were all having dinner together. That was what Oliver and I were discussing on the sidewalk." She admitted, shame coloring her face.

"You should have told me then. You should have told me any time after that, Josephine."

"I know. I'm so sorry. I just…I didn't have the heart to tell you. To be honest, I didn't even expect to see you again after. But then you were there and I was so happy to be with you. Being with you was so easy, Daniel. I'm so sorry. Oliver tried to warn me, but I was stubborn."

Danny breathed a sigh of relief.

"Okay, that's not so bad. Just call him and tell him that you found someone else. Tell him that you're going to marry me instead."

"He refuses to speak to me. I've been trying to get in touch with him from that day. And since being part of your world, I've doubled my efforts but he has not returned any of my calls, choosing only to relay messages to me via Oliver. I don't know what else to do."

"Okay, don't worry. How about we talk to the guy you're supposed to be marrying. Who is he? Maybe you can talk him out of the arrangement?"

"My father hasn't disclosed who it is. Oliver has been trying to use some contacts to find out but nothing has come up, no one will disclose any information. Besides, it will probably be a powerful ally or someone just as important so that if I refused, it will only ruin my reputation further." Josephine replied, bitterness seeping into her voice.

"He can't make you marry someone you've never even met!" Danny muttered, angrily stalking back and forth. Josephine stilled him with a touch of her hand on his bicep. She gazed up at him, lovingly. He spared her a tender ghost of a smile, placing his hand over hers.

"Oh, Daniel, I hate that I've dragged you into this. I was so selfish. You made me so happy. All of you do. Even Oliver has grown accustomed to your family and that's unheard of really."

"Then stay. We'll work it out somehow. Your Dad will realize you mean business when you don't go back." Danny said, imploringly. She closed her eyes at his words, and turned back to face the window.

Chapter Nine

"I have to go back, Daniel. I'm part of the royal family and it will be so much worse if I don't go back. I have responsibilities to the crown, I have responsibilities to him. He is my king as well as my father...Please Daniel, try to understand. I don't want this either."

Danny spun her around to face him. "I'm trying to understand. I really am, but I can't. Tell me what you could have done so wrong that he would basically disown you and now issue an ultimatum marriage?"

Josephine shook her head "No. I couldn't bear reliving the worst time of my life. I don't want to see the disappointment and disgust in your eyes like I saw in my father's."

"Please tell me, Josephine. Nothing you could say will change my heart. It belongs to you and it always will."

Her eyes shone with unshed tears as she bit her lip in worry.

"Okay." she whispered in a tiny voice. Danny kissed the palm of her hand and led her to couch.

"We don't normally do arranged marriages in our family, especially not when your chance at taking the throne is very slim, as in my case. We usually get to choose our own suitable partners when we reach 25 and that's what I thought I did."

Have Love

Josephine crossed her legs and stared at their hands clasped together, her gracefully thin brown fingers intertwined with his pale cream ones. She gave his hand one last squeeze before speaking.

"His name was Gustav and he was a school friend whom my family adored. I wasn't particularly in love with him but he was very suitable and it pleased my father. He runs our country's leading newspaper and magazine like his own father before him. So when he asked, I said yes. I never sought fairytales, so I didn't believe in happily after endings. I didn't thinking falling madly in love with someone was possible until I met you. But I was willing to have a quiet life with a person I believed to have my best interests at heart."

"I'm guessing that wasn't entirely accurate?" Danny gently inquired.

"No, not in the slightest. I found this out the day after we went on a short trip to Switzerland. We had separate hotel rooms, of course, so I went to mine to get changed for dinner after an afternoon of skiing. I had only taken off my, how do you call it…ugh, the word escapes me... my overalls and sweater when two photographers burst into the room and started taking pictures of me in my state of undress. I later found out that Gustav arranged this to happen by bribing the concierge at the front desk to give him a copy of my room card. Oliver did his very best to retrieve the data but by then Gustav had printed it as front page news. For weeks, you couldn't pick up a paper in Austria without seeing me in my underwear splashed all over it, talking about how hot to trot I was or that I was planning to pose for Penthouse or some other disgusting lie."

"That sounds horrible."

"The worst part was that my father blamed me for it. That I allowed myself to be photographed in such a vulnerable state, that I chose poorly for a future addition to our royal house. My brothers and their families refused to speak to me as well in a show of solidarity. I don't know if I wouldn't have left on my own if my father hadn't banished me to Bridgeville. I was so unhappy, I cried every day during that month. Only Oliver's faith in me never wavered. It was a reprieve to be able to come here far away from it all."

"I'm so sorry, Josephine." She spared him a weak smile.

"At least Gustav has been sued to bankruptcy and will never work in Austria ever again. That was the only light in this story."

"None of this is your fault. If you could just speak to your dad, if you could just explain to him what happened..."

"It's too late, Daniel. It's much too late." Josephine choked out a sob, trying bravely to keep the tears at bay.

"What do you mean it's too late? What do you mean?"

"I have to leave tonight. My father sent a private jet that leaves in the next 3 hours. The wedding will be on Christmas Day. I'm so sorry, Daniel. I only found out on my way here to meet Gwen. I called Daniella already so don't worry, I would never leave Gwen without supervision."

"What about Gwen? She's going to be destroyed if you go now."

"I told her I was going away for a little while. That's how we ended up with her listening to my poor judgment at including a child into adult affairs."

"She'll be fine, okay sure, but what about us? What we have is a once in a life time kind of thing" Danny exclaimed, miserably.

"I don't want to marry him, Daniel but I have to. It is my duty and I have to follow through." Josephine gave up fighting the tears, her face crumbling at having to say those words.

"You can't go, Josephine. You belong here with me." he held her face in his hands, kissing her endlessly as their streaming tears intermingled, tasting the salty-sweet on her lips.

"I do. I belong with you. I wish so very much that I could stay, but my heart will forever be yours, Daniel. It will be with you always, no matter what."

"You can't. Please. We can work this out together." Danny pleaded. The doorbell rang incessantly, purposefully intruding on their moment.

"I wish we could with all of my heart, Daniel. That's Oliver at the door. I have to go now or else he'll break down the door to find me. I don't think Daniella would be pleased about that." Josephine said breathlessly, their foreheads touching, as she slowly pulled away from him.

"I'll come with you. I'll go to Austria and we'll get your father's approval. We can fix this."

Her fingers fluttered to his lips in the barest of touches.

"If he would give you a chance, I know he would love you almost as much as I do."

"Good. Then I'll go with you..."

"You can't leave your life here, Daniel. You know that. Your bookstore and your sister, and what about Gwen? She needs you to keep her mother sane."

Danny chuckled despite of himself. He knew she was right but he didn't care at that moment, he just knew that he needed to be with her.

"Give me your father's number, I'll call him myself. I'll make him see sense. We'll give Daniella's his number at let her wear him down. We have options, Josephine."

"I wish it was that simple. I really do."

"Then let's do that. You don't have to go."

"You know I do." She whispered against his lips one final time.

The doorbell's incessant ringing resumed.

"Have a Happy Christmas, Danny. I love you." Josephine took a deep breath, and stood to her full height as if she'd gathered all of her strength, all of her aristocratic breeding, into that one motion. She touched her fingertips to his chest and swiftly walked out of the house.

Danny ran after her but Oliver had bundled her away into the back of the taxi by the time he reached outside. Oliver spared him a sympathetic smile and climbed in the seat beside her. Josephine twisted in her seat until she could face him from the rear window. She stared at him as tears poured down her face and, like that, she was gone in a sea of holiday season traffic.

Chapter Ten

"You can't mope on Christmas Eve, Danny. She made her decision. You should accept it and move on." Daniella lectured as they sat on her living room floor, wrapping last minute gifts.

"That wasn't a decision. It was an ultimatum. He didn't give her much choice and I don't think you would have chosen that differently if the shoe was on the other foot"

"I don't know. Maybe you're right. Don't get me wrong, I really liked her and I thought you two were great together, but she's been gone three days now without any word. I think that's saying something."

"I'm not going to give up on her. I won't. And where is all of your Christmas miracle talk now that I need it, huh?" Danny glared at his sister, who glared right back.

"I would have gone to Austria if this damn blizzard hadn't grounded all international flights. Instead I'm stuck here, going crazy, and I'll more than likely ruin Christmas by openly weeping at the dinner table."

Daniella shook her head knowing that he wasn't exaggerating too much. Taking stock of his raggedy three day old beard that he couldn't be bothered to shave since the morning after Josephine left him, and his tired, bloodshot eyes, her heart broke for him.

"Danny, is there anything that Rick and I could do? Anything that we can do to help ease your suffering?"

"Brain removal maybe? I don't know. I just wish I could talk to her or something, try to reason with her, but there's no number for royal palace of Austria in any phonebook. Ugh, I hate this. I feel so helpless. I just miss her, you know? I miss the sound of her voice." He admitted, miserably.

"I know, honey. It'll be okay."

"I'll tell you something right now, though. This Luther Vandross Christmas CD that you're playing is definitely not helping."

Daniella laughed and threw a few bows at her brother.

"Okay, wrapping is complete. Should we put Rick out of his misery and let him and Gwen come back downstairs now?"

"Yeah, sounds good. You put away the presents and I'll make some hot cocoa."

"Deal. We can watch a holiday movie or something to take your mind off of things."

"We can try." Danny agreed without much conviction as he got to his feet and helped her up. Daniella sighed as she watched his plaid shirt and jean clad form retreat into the kitchen.

A few minutes later, the doorbell rang while Danny stirred the chocolate beverage on the stove, absentmindedly splashing it all over the range. His thoughts were thousands of miles away, so much so that he barely heard Daniella calling his name. He looked up to find his sister staring at him with her hands on her hips.

"Didn't you hear me? I said you have a guest."

"I do? Is it Jack Frost? That's the only person who'd show up in the middle of a frigging snowstorm." He muttered, dejectedly.

"You're so melodramatic." Daniella's eyes wandered over to the mess he'd made on the stove and scowled at him before turning on her heels and stalking out. Danny frowned, wiping his hands on a dish towel, wondering who could it be when she appeared before him in the doorway.

"Josephine?"

"Hello, Daniel."

"You're really here? I'm not having some kind of hallucination?"

"No. I'm really here. I've missed you..." She confessed, timidly. Danny's face broke into a beaming smile as he rushed forward to sweep her up into his arms in a big swirling hug that had her squealing in delight. She laughed, kissing him until he set her back onto unsteady feet but didn't let her out of his arms.

"How did you get here? Please tell me you didn't get on a plane? You shouldn't have flown in dangerous weather like this!"

"It was entirely too dangerous to fly, of course. So we landed in the closest place where there were no blizzard or snow storms, which was Virginia. Then, we took a Greyhound bus, and then rented a car. Have you ever traveled via Greyhound before, Daniel? It's marvelous! You meet so many lovely people. I'll admit some of them are quite handsy…"

"You did all that to come see me? Wait, what about your father and the arranged wedding?"

"The entire flight back home, I couldn't stop thinking about you. I couldn't bear to think of being with anyone else. So as soon as I landed in Austria, I met with my father and called the whole thing off."

"Oh Thank God! You're the best Christmas present ever." Josephine stole a kiss as soon as he said those words.

"So did you get him to finally listen and admit that he was wrong? Did he accept you back with open arms because he realized he was being stubborn?"

"I know we believe in Christmas miracles, Daniel, but let's take it easy! My father hasn't changed his mind exactly, but he's listened to my side for the first time. I told him about us and why I couldn't marry his preference for my suitor. His name was Roderick and he's a very prominent military man in one of our allied countries, by the way. In the end I informed him that I wished to relinquish my claim to the throne, my titles and resign from my post as royal Hedge Fund analyst." Danny stared at her in shock.

"What? You did what?! And your father accepted that?"

"No. He told me to have a Happy Christmas and he'd see me on the fifteenth of January to discuss my future." Josephine replied, sheepishly.

"No way."

"Oh, and he wants you to be there, as well."

"Me? Your father, the king, wants to meet me?" Danny wore a cartoonish expression that had Josephine smiling fondly at him. She'd missed him more than she'd ever realized was humanly possible.

"Well, you did say you wanted to marry me." Josephine quipped, batting her eyes at him.

"Oh yeah, I did say that, didn't I? Well, are you free today?" Danny said as he pulled Josephine back into his arms. She giggled at the ticklish feel against her cheek as his prickly unshaved face rubbed against hers.

"I wouldn't anger royalty, if I were you, Darling."

"You called me 'Darling'! We're official?" She nodded, beaming at him.

"So are you going to kiss me or not?"

"Gladly." Danny cupped her face in his hands and gazed lovingly into her eyes, whispering against her eagerly awaiting lips.

"Merry Christmas, Princess."

More Great Books

The Trouble with Playing Cupid
Book 1, The Cupid Series
by Tamara Philip

One New Year's Eve, shy singer, December Brown drunkenly texts her talk show host pal, Trace Randall, about her long time crush on the aloof actor, Tom Elmswood. Thinking the two celebrities would make a cute couple, he unwisely decides to play matchmaker... in front of a live studio audience.

Things start to go downhill when Tom admits he's never even heard of December before. Now what seemed like a sure fire hit quickly becomes a flop. Will these two lonely hearts ever make a love connection or has this cupid's arrow missed its mark?

Tamara Philip

NOMINATED for
Outstanding Debut Author
in Interracial Romance 2015

After spending most of her life in New York City, Tamara Philip decided to let love lead her on an international adventure, where she's met many amazing people and ate entirely too much. Tamara and her English-born fiance, Chris, now split their time between the United Kingdom and The Caribbean.

The Trouble with Playing Cupid was her debut novel, and *The Trouble with Romance*, Book 2 in the Cupid Series. Writing has been her secret passion since childhood. Quirky female leads are her trademark.

On any given day you can find Tamara telling people what to do, dodging wedding planning, and working hard on her next novel.

Where to find Tamara Philip online

Website: TamaraPhilipWrites.wordpress.com
Twitter: @MsTamaraPhilip
Facebook: https://www.facebook.com/TamaraPhilipwrites